DATE DUE			
JAN 02			
FEB 16 02			
MAY 07 02	JUL 02		
NOV 22 02			
MAY 02 03			
04/13/04			

12/00

JACKSON COUNTY
Library Services

HEADQUARTERS
413 West Main Street
Medford, Oregon 97501

HAGAR

*Also by James R. Shott
in Large Print:*

Joseph
Leah

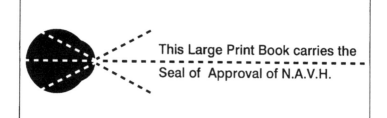

This Large Print Book carries the
Seal of Approval of N.A.V.H.

HAGAR

JAMES R. SHOTT

Thorndike Press • Thorndike, Maine

Published in 2000 by arrangement with Herald Press,
a division of Mennonite Publishing House, Inc.

Thorndike Press Large Print Christian Fiction Series.

The tree indicium is a trademark of Thorndike Press.

The text of this Large Print edition is unabridged.
Other aspects of the book may vary from the original edition.

Set in 16 pt. Plantin by PerfecType.

Printed in the United States on permanent paper.

Library of Congress Cataloging-in-Publication Data

Shott, James R., 1925–
   Hagar / James R. Shott.
      p. cm.
    ISBN 0-7862-2862-8 (lg. print : hc : alk. paper)
     1. Hagar (Biblical character)—Fiction. 2. Bible. O.T.—
  History of Biblical events—Fiction. 3. Women in the Bible
  —Fiction. 4. Large type books. I. Title.
PS3569.H598 H3 2000
  813′.54—dc21
                                                  00-059962

To Kathy, Connie and Shirley,
my three favorite daughters,
whom I not only love,
but like and admire.

1

The slave market in Haran came alive with the sunrise. Everyone knew the best slaves would be sold early, and by midmorning only the sick and rebellious ones remained.

In one stall near the center of the market, a naked child stood with her master waiting to be sold. She was pretty, in a childlike way. Her long dark hair, round face, and smooth tawny skin meant that as an adult she would be a beauty. The only other person in the stall was her master, who was eagerly waiting for a suitable buyer.

The girl had restless eyes. They darted everywhere. She watched as an Egyptian slave trader made his way through the tangle of stalls and booths, purchasing slaves for re-sale in another city. With him were his fore-man and seven roughlooking guards bearing staves. As he went from stall to stall, he purchased many. Soon his string of slaves numbered twenty, shuffling along in chains.

The girl with the restless eyes watched as the trader came to a stall in which a strong man stood naked and alone in the center of the stall. The man's wiry body proclaimed him a good worker. His erect bearing probably meant he was a freeman, now forced into slavery because of his debts. Attesting to this were the other two men in the stall, armed and threatening — the creditors.

"Field hand," muttered the foreman in Egyptian. He looked the slave over. "Farmer, I'd say. Fatten him up, and he would bring a pretty profit in Mari or Babylon."

The slave trader nodded. "Offer them twenty silver."

To their surprise, the offer was accepted. The two creditors divided the coins greedily. The man was then chained to the other slaves, making their count now twenty-one.

The stall next to the girl contained a slave family. The man glowered, although his hard muscled body advertised his strength. His wife was stooped with age, her breasts sagging, her skin mottled. The two voluptuous teenaged girls stood tall, swaying their hips provocatively.

The slave trader smiled. "I know a brothel in Babylon," he said, "where these two girls would bring double what we'll pay for them here."

"Don't buy the man," said the foreman. "His back is scarred."

"The old woman is no good either." The trader produced his purse. "Try to get the girls for thirty silver total."

The girl with the restless eyes shuddered. She had heard and understood the Egyptian conversation.

The foreman, who spoke the local dialect, bargained with the owner of the family. Finally a reasonable price was settled: twenty silver for each of the daughters. The trader counted out the money. The girls joined the others, their bold eyes flashing invitations to the leering guards. The father and mother, broken by too much pain, now seemed unconcerned at the breaking up of their family.

They came to the next stall, where the girl had been watching them. She shrank as their eyes probed her. She was used to nudity, but their gaze made her feel dirty.

"That brothel in Babylon," said the slave trader in Egyptian. "Would they take someone this young?"

The foreman snorted. "Take her! They'd pay twice as much as they would for those other two! She's undoubtedly a virgin, and lots of their customers would pay big money to spoil a child!"

The girl shuddered. The last time she was on the trading block four years ago, she had heard about "perpetual virgins" who were trained to simulate virginity over and over again. Although only six years old at the time, she understood and was horrified.

The slave trader looked sharply at her, his eyes narrowed. "Ask her master how old she is."

Before the foreman could ask, the child spoke in fluent Egyptian. "I'm fourteen, sir."

"I thought she was Egyptian! She looks like one." The trader's eyes widened. "Fourteen, did you say?"

"Yes, sir."

He looked at her flat chest and narrow hips.

"You look about nine."

"Well . . . sir. . . . You see, sir . . . the sickness. . . ."

"Sickness? What sickness?"

But the girl stared at her feet and would say no more.

"Acch!" The foreman spat. "Don't buy her! You can't tell what she has!"

The two men backed away, then hurried on to the next stall.

The master confronted his child slave.

"What did you say to them?" he demanded harshly.

The girl would not look at her master. "They — they asked me how old I was. I told them fourteen."

"Fourteen! But — you're only ten!"

"Yes, sir. I . . . I told them it was because of the sickness — "

"What! What sickness?" The man's forehead creased in a dark frown. "You just lost me a sale! Why did you do that?"

"They . . . they wanted me for a brothel in Babylon."

"Oh." The master's face softened. Suddenly he threw back his head and laughed. "Fourteen! The sickness! Ah, child, you are a smart one! By Yarah, I ought to let you sell yourself! You seem to be picking out your own future master!"

"Let me, Master! I promise I'll get the best price for you! Just let me do it myself! Please?"

"Why not? It's worth a try." He stepped outside the stall, but close enough to see and hear everything.

A fat middle-aged man stepped into the stall. Under his thick brows his eyes gleamed as he stared at the naked girl before him. His hands clenched and opened nervously. He pursed his lips; a small drivel of saliva ran down his short beard.

"Ah! Ah! That is what I want. Exactly!"

He reached out to touch her chest; she cringed.

"Come on, girl! I've got a right to — "

The master stepped into the stall and pushed him away. "You've got no right to manhandle the merchandise. Keep your slimy hands off!"

The customer stepped back, eyes widening. "But she's only a slave!" he whined. "I got a right to — ah, never mind. How much is she?"

"Sixty silver."

"Sixty? What is she, made of solid gold? I'll give you twenty for her."

"No. Sixty. That's it."

The man shook his head. "I can get three like her for sixty."

"Then go get 'em!" barked the master.

The man turned and shuffled out.

The girl turned to her master. "Thank you, sir," she murmured.

The master frowned at his young slave. "I'd never — " He shook his head. "Do you still want to sell yourself?"

"Yes sir. Only . . . please stay close by."

The master nodded and stepped just outside the booth.

The next person to step into the stall was a woman of classic beauty. Her face was

accented by high cheekbones, dark eyebrows, and red painted lips. She wore
Babylonian-style clothing — high tiara, cop-
per frontlet, long light blue linen dress,
fringed in gold at the bottom and bound at
the waist with a gold sash. She held her head
high, her shoulders squared.

The slave girl smiled. "Good morning, my
lady."

The wealthy woman smiled back. "Well,"
she said, her voice musically soft, "you certainly are cheerful for a slave!"

"I have a lot to be cheerful about," said
the girl. "I think I'm about to be bought by
the most beautiful woman in Haran!"

The lady chuckled. "And why should I
buy you?"

"Because I am obedient, intelligent, beautiful . . . and very humble!"

The lady laughed heartily. "I can't imagine you as a slave. You certainly don't act like
one."

"My master," she indicated the man out-
side the stall, "has allowed me to sell myself.
I am authorized to strike a bargain with you.
Now how much do you offer for me?"

"And what do you think you're worth?"
asked the lady, her eyes twinkling.

"Just a moment ago a man was here to
buy me. My master set a price of sixty silver.

The buyer turned it down. He wasn't smart; I'm worth at least sixty. Besides, I promised my master I would bring a good price for myself."

The lady shook her head in disbelief. "I can't believe this! Never have I — " She turned to the master outside the stall. "Is this true? Is she permitted to do all this herself?"

"She is, my lady," said the master. He was shrewd enough to say no more.

"In that case. . . ." The lady looked again at the girl. She rubbed her chin. "I'll pay you sixty silver. Agreed?"

The master caught his breath. "That much?" He recovered and practically ran into the stall. "Agreed. Agreed. By all means!"

The lady counted out the coins into a small bag. Before she handed it over, she said, "But she will have to be clothed. Surely she wore something when you brought her to the market?"

"Yes, yes, of course, my lady." The master went to the pack he had hung on a peg at the back of the booth. "I have a dress here. Yes. Yes. Right here."

He produced a worn woolen robe and threw it to the girl. She hurriedly slipped it on.

"Now," said the lady as she handed the purse of coins to the master. "You're mine. What do you think of that?"

The girl smiled. "Wonderful! What shall I call you, my lady?"

"Sarai. Sarai *isha* Abram *ben* Terah."

"Terah?" The girl's eyes opened wide. "That rich herdsman from Ur? Really?"

The woman nodded. "And what shall I call you?"

The girl still stared at her new mistress. She drew a deep breath, swallowed, and said, "Hagar."

"Hagar? That's an Egyptian name, isn't it?"

"Yes, ma'am. My parents were Egyptian."

"Well, come along, Hagar the Egyptian." She reached out her hand and took the girl's in a firm grasp. "Let's get out of here before someone else wants to buy you!"

They hurried away giggling, leaving behind a bewildered former master counting the unexpected largess from his sale. He glanced after them. They looked to him more like mother and daughter than mistress and slave.

He shook his head, shrugged, and went back to his counting.

2

Outside the slave booth, seven men waited. Their bearded faces, long burnooses, and shepherd staffs seemed out of place in this setting. When Sarai went to them, Hagar knew they were household guards. Their innocent looking shepherd staffs were actually weapons.

"Mardi," said Sarai to one of them, a middle-aged man with the short pointed beard of a Babylonian. "This is Hagar."

The man leered at her. Sarai hastily added, "She's a virgin, and she will stay that way."

The man frowned, but nodded meekly. "Yes, my lady," he mumbled.

Sarai, still clutching Hagar's hand, led the way and the guards followed. They passed through the slave market with its dispirited prisoners in booths or stalls, on blocks, or standing brazenly in an open space. There were families, single men, young girls, young boys, and even babies. All were naked; all looked defeated. Hagar breathed a sigh of relief, aware of her good fortune.

Having lived in Haran for four years, Hagar knew the city was known primarily for its markets, including agriculture, trade goods from all over the world, and of course slaves. They passed the temple of Yarah, which marked the beginning of the business district. Hagar glanced without regret at the *ziggurat,* its dark zigzag steps silhouetted against the blue sky. On its height she had spent many moonlit nights worshiping the moon god.

As they walked, Sarai quizzed her new possession.

"Tell me about yourself. Have you always been a slave?"

Hagar shook her head. "Only for the last five years. Before that, my family was free."

"How did you become slaves?"

"Father's farm in Egypt failed; he was forced to sell his freedom."

"Did they break up your family?"

"Yes. They sold Father first, then Mother with her baby. Then me."

"That must have been a hard time for you."

"It was, my lady. We didn't know they

were going to do that. It was one of the conditions Father insisted on when he agreed to slavery to pay our debts. Our creditors didn't care; they sold out to the first one to bid on Father."

"Did he submit willingly?"

"No. I can remember that vividly. They dragged Father away unconscious. There was blood everywhere. I can still hear Mother's screams."

Sarai sighed. "And then they took your mother?"

"Yes, with the baby. Something about needing a wet nurse."

"I see. Yes, that would bring a good price."

It did not take them long to pass through the residential section with its cone-shaped mud houses and outdoor kitchens. They followed the River Balikh through several markets. Hagar had seen it all before. She scarcely glanced at the displays of cloth, wines, jewelry, weapons, and spices whose fragrances hinted of far away and mysterious places.

Sarai waited until they had passed the noisy throngs before she resumed her questioning. "So you were the only one in your family left on the slave block. What did they do with you?"

"I was purchased by a slave trader. He

took me away from Egypt and sold me about a year later here in Haran."

"That must have been an awful year for you."

"It was, my lady. I cried most of that year."

Sarai spoke softly. "You're so cheerful now. How did you ever recover from that horrid experience?"

"Another slave helped me. She said I could die of grief or put it behind me and live. The choice was in my hands. I decided to live."

"You made that choice when you were four?" Sarai stared at her slave wide-eyed.

"Five, my lady. Between four and five, I grew up."

"Yes, I believe it. No wonder you're mature beyond your years. Now tell me about your last owner. Was he good to you?"

"Yes, very good. He is a merchant in Haran. He bought me for his son, who was my age. I was going to be his . . . sexual companion when he was old enough."

"But why did he . . . ?"

"About a month ago, the boy became ill with the fever and died. My master had no use for me then, so he sold me today."

"I see." Sarai walked silently beside her new slave.

Only a slight pressure on her hand gave Hagar any indication of her new mistress's thoughts. They continued walking, coming at last to a group of black tents.

"Here is your new home, Hagar." Sarai dismissed her guards with a nod and went toward the largest tent in the village. "We must be quiet. Terah may be sleeping."

Hagar shivered in anticipation. Soon she would meet her new family — the patriarch Terah, one of the wealthiest men in all Padan-Aram, and his son Abram, husband of her mistress. And who else?

Just as they were about to enter the tent, a young man came out. He was tall, his curly brown hair haloing a beardless face. Hagar estimated his age at about four or five years more than her own. His bold eyes looked her over, up and down. For a moment she felt as though she were still standing naked on the slave block.

"Ah!" the youth exclaimed, his thin lips curling. "Aunt Sarai's new *amah*. Very nice!"

"This is my nephew, Lot," said Sarai hastily. "Lot, this is my new *shifkhah*."

She seemed to place a small emphasis on the word *shifkhah*. The word meant "hand-maid," a personal servant. This implied special privileges. It warmed Hagar to know that at least she hadn't said *amah*, the usual word for a common female slave. But perhaps the emphasis on the carefully selected word was a warning to Lot. Yet why would such a warning be necessary? Hagar glanced at Lot. His handsome face broke into a challenging grin.

"Aw, Aunt Sarai, you didn't have to say that. You know I wouldn't — "

"Why aren't you with your flock?" Sarai demanded.

"I came to pay my respects to Grandfather Terah," the young man replied. "Father Abram says he's very weak."

"Where is Abram?"

"Over there." Lot jerked his head toward an adjoining tent, and then flung a saucy grin at Hagar. "I'll see you later, *shifkhah*."

The way he used the word was almost taunting. Hagar decided she didn't like this brash youth. She would avoid him as much as possible.

As he trotted away, Sarai glanced after him, shaking her head. "The boy's father is dead, and he's living with us. I hope Abram doesn't take him along when we move. But I suppose we'll have to."

"Move?" Hagar felt enough confidence in her new mistress to ask a bold question. "Why are you moving?"

Sarai shrugged. "Oh, I don't know. Abram

21

thinks his God has told him to go to some new country. I don't know why we can't stay here. This is as good a land as any, and our family has settled here."

She waved her hand across the cluster of tents and cone shaped homes. Evidently the household of Terah lived in both tents and houses. Hagar could understand the tents, but why the more permanent mud and brick buildings? Were some planning to move and some to stay? If so, how many would move?

Her questions would have to wait, however. Sarai was kicking off her sandals. She led Hagar into the tent.

The large interior was ornately furnished. The carpet under Hagar's now bare feet was soft and comforting. Chests and tables and tapestries and lamps surrounded her in an organized clutter. She caught a whiff of incense in the air. It was sweet, musty, and at the same time faintly medicinal.

In the center of the tent lay the old patriarch, propped up on pillows. His bony feet stuck out at the bottom of the plain linen garment he wore. The face in the white hair and beard was sharp and surprisingly free of wrinkles. His clear eyes watched the two newcomers from under white eyebrows.

"Father Terah," said Sarai softly. "This is my new *shifkhah*. Her name is Hagar. She comes from Egyptian parentage."

The old man nodded. "Come closer, child."

Hagar knelt by his side. During the past four years of servitude, she had served her master's aging father until his death. She knew something of how to care for a dying man.

"How may I serve you, Grandfather Terah?"

She used the same term of respect Lot had used, but without Lot's arrogance. Even a slave could call aging patriarchs "Grandfather" if the slave belonged to the family.

A small smile fluttered on Terah's lips. "Wine," he said. He nodded toward the small table nearby, on which stood a decanter and cups.

Hagar poured half a cup, then held it for him to drink. When he had finished, she reached for a clean cloth on the table and wiped his lips.

"Thank you, child," he murmured.

She replaced the cup on the table and was about to stand, but he caught her hand. She stayed on her knees and looked at him expectantly.

Although he kept his eyes on Hagar, Terah spoke to Sarai. "Is this the one, daughter?"

"This is the one, Father," replied Sarai.

The old man's eyes traveled over the girl. "She's very young."

Sarai replied, "I won't need her for at least five years."

"Do you think you can keep her safe that long?"

"Yes, Father. You may be sure of it."

Hagar felt uncomfortable, although she could not begin to understand what they were talking about. She only knew they were talking about her, almost as though she were a sheep or a goat.

The old man chuckled. "You don't know what this is all about, do you, child? Well, you'll know soon enough. And you're Egyptian? Do you speak Egyptian?"

"Yes, Grandfather."

"Good. My son might need an interpreter if he travels to the west as he intends. Although I think he's foolish to do that." He snorted. "He thinks he has found some strange new God. I think our *teraphim*, our household gods, are good enough for our family. We've carried them with us and worshiped them for several generations now, and they've served us well."

Terah still held Hagar's hand. He gripped it a little tighter and looked into her eyes.

"What god do you worship, girl?"

Hagar hesitated. She did not want to offend the family patriarch, but she had always been completely honest with her masters. So she replied boldly.

"Grandfather, I have no god at all. My former master wanted me to worship Yarah, but I couldn't."

"Could you worship a God you can't even see?"

Hagar wondered why she was being questioned this way. But honesty compelled her to reply.

"I suppose I can worship an invisible God as well as one I can see."

The old man stared at her silently for a moment, considering her ambiguous answer. Then he nodded. "I think," he said slowly, "that you will believe what you want to believe, and not follow blindly the gods of your masters." He smiled. "But that's enough talk of gods for today."

Terah looked up at Sarai who had remained standing through the entire conversation. "Take good care of this one, daughter. She's intelligent, beautiful, and charming. She will be perfect for what you need."

There it was again, that vague reference to Hagar and her purpose as Sarai's slave. She hoped her mistress would tell her about that soon.

Terah dropped her hand, so she assumed the interview was over. She rose and bowed deeply, speaking the words of farewell. Then she followed Sarai out of the tent.

"Now you must meet Abram," said Sarai.

3

Abram was not in his tent. Hagar was impressed with the ordered clutter in the interior — saddle bags filled with household gear, small light-weight furniture, rolls of carpets and tapestries. Yet the hodgepodge was neat and organized, as though ready to move to a new camp at any time.

"Just as soon as Terah is well," Sarai explained, seeing Hagar's interest in the well-packed gear. "We're moving westward."

"Because Abram's new God told him to move?"

"Yes." Sarai shook her head slowly. "I just don't understand . . . but Abram is so sure."

"Has this God really spoken to him? An invisible God? How could — "

"I don't know, child. I'm not sure Abram does either. But he certainly believes it. He's not exactly a fanatic; he's more of a . . . a . . . ."

"Dreamer?"

Sarah nodded vigorously. "Exactly. A mystic. But he's still a good businessman. As good as old Terah; better than his brother Nahor. His flocks and herds — "

A voice from the door of the tent interrupted her. "I seem to be the object of this discussion. May I join it?"

Hagar swung around and looked at the man who had just come in. He was of medium height, heavily bearded, his curly brown hair long and sleek with oil. His tanned wrinkle-free face reminded her of Terah. He shared the family characteristic of swarthy but smooth skin. He wore the long flowing burnoose of a shepherd.

What impressed Hagar most was his eyes. Sunken. Restless. Burning. The eyes of a fanatic? Or the eyes of an intelligent man, absorbing knowledge, thinking, exploring, wondering. At that moment, they bored into Hagar.

"Ah!" he said, his voice vibrant with energy. "This must be the new slave you went to purchase today."

Sarai nodded. "Her name is Hagar. She's an Egyptian."

"Egyptian? Good. We might need her later."

He strode briskly through the tent to stand before her. Hagar wondered if he would demand that she strip, as many new masters would have done. But Abram's eyes as they traveled over her body held no hint of lust, only interest.

"Tell me, child," he said, speaking in a low voice. "What gods do you worship?"

The first question from her new master would have been more of a surprise to Hagar had Sarai not told her Abram was a mystic and dreamer.

"Sir," she replied, speaking boldly, "I have no god. My former master wanted me to worship Yarah, but I could not."

"And why not?" demanded Abram.

Sarai threw up her hands and sighed. "Well, if you two are going to talk about the gods, I might as well speak to the servants about supper." She left the tent.

Abram seated himself on the carpet, motioning Hagar to a place beside him. She sank down on the soft rug and crossed her legs, facing him.

"Now tell me, girl," said Abram. "Why did you reject the moon goddess?"

She had long ago determined she would be totally honest with whatever master she served. Besides, she felt honored that Abram considered her adult enough to talk this way with her. Or — was he trying to convert her to his God?

"Sir," she said, "I enjoyed standing on the roof of the ziggurat each month, singing and praising the full moon. It was so beautiful. I did it gladly. But there was no god up there. Only the moon. He had no power. He had no way of telling us anything. It all seemed so silly to me. That thing up there was . . . well, nothing but a pretty moon."

Abram nodded. "And what would it take for you to believe in a god — any god?"

Hagar frowned, thinking about this. "I think he would have to speak to me. I don't know how. But I would have to be sure."

"Could you believe in God if he spoke to you through me?"

Here it comes, she thought. He was trying to lead her to his God. Sarai had said he was not a fanatic, just a dreamer, a mystic. But anyone who began a relationship with this kind of evangelistic pressure was, to her, a fanatic.

But she must be honest.

"No, sir, I could not. He must speak to me."

"Ah. I see." Abram frowned. After a moment he spoke again. "Assuming that he would speak to you, could you believe there is only one God, and thus all those other gods — like Yarah — do not exist?"

Now it was Hagar's turn to be silent for a moment. Finally she gathered her courage to ask the question which had been on her mind ever since Abram began to speak of his God.

"Yes, I could, sir," she said softly. "But may I ask you a question?"

"Yes, my dear. Ask anything you like."

"What is your God's name?"

Abram pressed his forefinger against his chin. "I don't know," he said slowly. "He has never told me."

His tolerance of her question encouraged her to ask another.

"Do you truly believe that your God is the only one?"

"Yes. Why do you ask?"

She hesitated, but she knew she would have to continue. "Because . . . you spoke of Gods, not God. *Elohim,* not *El.* Why do you call him that?"

Abram smiled, almost indulgently. "I see." He stroked his beard. "I say *Elohim* because God is the God of gods, and all gods are encompassed in his one being. He is only one, but so great he includes all."

Hagar wrinkled her forehead. "I don't understand."

Abram smiled. "Nor do I, child. There's so much I don't understand. That's the mystery and wonder of my God, who speaks to me in ways I cannot begin to comprehend."

"Please sir — I . . . well, first you tell me about a God I can't see. Now you are asking me to believe in a God I don't understand. How can I do that?"

Abram's voice was soft, caressing her. "Yes, my child. I am asking you to do just that. I have done it, and I find it is not too difficult. I would like to understand. I search for understanding. But even when I can't, I believe."

This was too confusing for Hagar to grasp. She shook her head and said as honestly as she could, "Father Abram, I just can't accept your God. He sounds too strange to me. I guess I'll just have to wait until he speaks to me directly."

The burning eyes studied her. Then he sighed. "All right, child. Perhaps some day he will come to you. I hope so. You have the wisdom and the maturity, even at your age, to be one of his special children."

Hagar had no idea what he was talking about. She wished this interview would end. She didn't want to be pressured into belief, and she was too honest to tell him she believed when she didn't.

Abram seemed to sense her withdrawal, for he leaned back on a cushion. "Ask Sarai to come to me," he said. "I want to talk with her."

Hagar rose and left the tent.

Was her master displeased with her, simply because she was honest? Should she perhaps tell him she believed in his strange religion even when she didn't? No. That's what all the other slaves would do. But not her. She would continue to be honest, despite the consequences. But she felt uncomfortable with her new master.

Sarai had called him a dreamer and a mystic. Hagar called him a fanatic.

4

"Hagar, wake up!"

Sarai's insistent whisper brought Hagar to consciousness. A soft glow of lamplight illumined the tent. Still at least an hour before dawn.

"What is it, Mother Sarai?"

She pushed back her tousled hair and sat up. Sarai stood and strode toward the door, saying as she went, "Father Terah is dying. Please hurry."

Hagar's throat constricted. During the two weeks since Sarai had purchased her from the slave market, she had come to love the old patriarch. She had spent several hours a day in his tent, feeding him, tending to his bodily needs, keeping him company. How easily she had become a part of the family! As though she had been here all her life, and the dying old man were her real grandfather.

She changed quickly from her sleeping robe, the one her former master had given her, and into the newer linen garment Sarai had provided. She ran a comb through her hair, then hurried after Sarai toward Terah's tent.

They were all there. Abram, Nahor and his wife Milcah, Lot, and several others. Abram looked up from his kneeling position beside Terah.

"He wants to speak to Hagar."

Hagar glanced around. Nobody else seemed as surprised as she. Evidently they had all had their turn to listen to the dying patriarch's words. Now it was Hagar's turn. That she would even have a turn, being a slave, a woman, and a newcomer to the family, surprised her.

She knelt on the carpet beside the old man's pallet. Terah's face appeared ashen in the lamplight. The smooth skin was deceiving; he looked many years younger and healthier than he was. The gasps through his open mouth gave the only indication that he was dying.

Hagar reached out and took the bony hand. The skin felt leathery to her.

"I'm here, Grandfather," she murmured.

Terah opened his eyes. With an effort he focused on her face. He wheezed in a deep breath, then let it rattle out.

"Hagar."

The words were faint. Hagar bent closer.

"Yes, Grandfather."

"Take good care . . . of my son."

For the past two weeks, no one had told her of her purpose in the household. Several times there had been hints, but when she asked for an explanation, they had merely muttered, "Later." Now another hint. Whatever her purpose was, it had to do with Abram.

"I will, Grandfather."

"May you . . . live long . . . and may your . . . womb be fruitful."

Hagar gently squeezed the hand. The formula blessing sounded sincere. She felt privileged that he would give it to a slave. But there was more.

"You will be . . . the mother . . . of a great nation."

It was customary for a dying patriarch to pronounce blessings and make predictions with his last breath. The predictions were valued and believed. He had probably done the same for many others in the tent. She still marveled that he would do it for her. They had grown close in the past two weeks, but she was still a slave.

Terah closed his eyes, and Hagar knew

that was all he would say. Now was the time for her to rise and go to the back of the tent, as a proper servant should. Instead she bent even closer and whispered in his ear.

"Grandfather, you are much loved. By everybody. By me. Die in peace."

With a final squeeze of the hand, she laid it down and stood. During this entire time, she had shed no tears. But now they came — quietly, softly, copiously. She stumbled to the back of the tent as Abram resumed his place beside the dying man.

Hers was the last blessing by the patriarch. Now they waited in silence for his death.

She knew from past experience that old men do not always die on schedule. Terah's ancient body continued to cling to life. In the silence she could hear, even from the back of the tent, the wheezing and rattling of his breathing. It could go on all day, she thought.

But it didn't, mercifully. Shortly after sunrise, she heard a long, slow wheeze, a loud rattle, then silence.

Abram, now kneeling beside his father, broke the stillness.

"Father Terah! Oh, Father Terah!"

With his signal, everyone in the tent began to wail and moan, offering respect to the just-departed patriarch by their noisy grief. Hagar heard the sound of ripping cloth. Her former master's household did not mourn by tearing their clothes, as her new family did. Perhaps their economic station had something to do with that. Terah's family could afford new garments.

She joined her voice with the others, and even tore her new linen robe. She tore it from the neck to the waist, according to the custom. Some of the people went even farther, tearing both above and below the belt to shreds. Patches of skin showed. Apparently, the more torn the garment, the more respect was shown.

She reached up to tear more, when suddenly she stopped. Lot was staring at her. She saw in his eyes something more than filial grief. Although he was moaning and wailing like all the others, the darting eyes went from one woman to another. She turned her back on him and did not tear her dress any further.

Now the family plodded out of the tent, leaving only Abram and Nahor to prepare the body for burial. Hagar sought out Sarai and clutched her hand. She noticed Sarai also had not torn her dress more than a token rip in the front. Had she too noticed Lot's roving eyes?

They sat on the dusty ground, because mourning customs forbade sitting on carpets or benches. They dirtied their faces and clothes. And always they continued to wail and groan. The entire camp-city mourned, and the keening and loud lamentation created a constant din.

No one did any work, except the necessary chores of watching the sheep and goats. No food would be eaten this day.

The sun rose in the sky; the day grew hot and uncomfortable. The combination of sweat and dust all over her body became unbearably itchy. Hagar noticed several women expressing their grief by slapping themselves. She did this herself on some of her prickling spots, finding some relief. But she felt guilty about easing her discomfort.

In the late afternoon, Abram and Nahor came out of the tent, bearing a stretcher with their father's body prepared for burial. The patriarch was dressed in an ornate linen robe, with sandals on his feet. The head was bare, but the hair was combed and oiled — in contrast to his two sons, who were properly disheveled in their grief.

All in the community instantly increased their wailing as they fell into place in the funeral procession. The intensity of sound became a roar as all competed to outdo each other in honoring their beloved patriarch. As they marched, they scooped up dust and flung it into the air.

Hagar's throat hurt from the constant bawling, but she kept it up, offering respect to her beloved grandfather. She constantly coughed, but so did everyone else, from the dust and the heat and the wailing.

The funeral procession wound for an hour into the surrounding hills to the tomb which Abram and Nahor had already prepared for their father. The shallow natural cave had been chipped out and a large crypt made ready to receive the body. This would be the family burial tomb for the clan as long as they remained in Haran.

Abram and Nahor and a few other men entered the cavern, leaving the others outside. They continued their babble of grief as best they could, although it had now died down to a hoarse moan. When Abram and the others finally emerged about an hour later, the women were almost unable to speak. At that moment, the wailing ceased, and the mourning became silent.

Now, thought Hagar, came the time of real mourning. The outward display of emotion showing respect was over. Now began the inner sorrow. The sorrow of silence.

The procession returning to the tents was

slow and mournful. Custom demanded that no one speak until the next morning, unless it was absolutely necessary.

Hagar clung to Sarai during that painful journey home. Sarai cried silently, as did Hagar; for both of them grief was a deep and real companion. Although they could not speak to each other, they comforted themselves by holding hands tightly.

Hagar slept with her mistress that night, as Sarai could not lie with Abram. They slept with blankets on the ground, and the dampness and cold added to their discomfort. Hagar, being younger, managed to sleep soundly through the night.

When Hagar awoke in the morning, Sarai had already gone to prepare food for the day. The thirty days of mourning would continue. But at least they could now eat and talk, as well as bathe and change clothing.

Hagar folded her blanket and smoothed her hair. She could not oil it, but she could comb it, and she went into the tent in search of a comb.

Lot was there.

"Good morning," he said, grinning.

Instinctively, she clutched her torn dress and held the edges close across her chest. She nodded and muttered a civil "Good morning," then tried to push past him.

Lot caught her arm and swung her around. "Eat breakfast with me," he said.

She could not refuse him. They went outside to the cooking pots. Each ladled stew into a bowl. Lot led her behind the tent, where they sat on the ground to eat. Hagar crossed her legs carefully, wondering what the young man was leading up to.

"You didn't tear your dress very much," Lot said between mouthfuls. "Look at mine."

His robe had many rents, almost in rags. One shoulder was bare. The bottom hem looked as though it had been fringed. He had evidently torn it in neat patterns.

Her throat felt raw as the hot stew touched it. As hungry as she was, she could not eat. Perhaps she could after it cooled. She laid the bowl down.

"Aren't you hungry?" he asked.

"It hurts my throat," she croaked. Even those few words caused pain.

She was glad she had laid aside her bowl. As his eyes darted to the front of her dress, she again reached up with both hands to pull the torn pieces together. She wondered why he would want to look at her; her chest was flat.

"What did Grandfather Terah say to you just before he died?" he asked.

She swallowed, trying to moisten her

throat. "The usual blessing," she said.

"And what did you say to him?"

She shook her head. "Nothing. Just . . . die in peace."

He looked at her steadily for a long moment before saying, "Is that all? What about me and Abram?"

"Well, you see — "

"Lot." Sarai stood before them, frowning. "Shouldn't you be with your flock?"

"Aw, Aunt Sarai — "

"Come, Hagar. We have work to do."

She reached out and grasped Hagar's hand, pulling her to her feet. Hagar followed gratefully, wanting to get away from the young man with the roving eyes, even if it meant leaving her bowl of stew behind on the ground. They went around the tent to where several women were cleaning up the breakfast remains.

Hagar noticed Lot shuffling off toward the plain where the flocks grazed. She glanced at Sarai.

"I left my bowl of stew back there. I'll get it."

Sarai nodded. Hagar went around the tent to pick up the bowl. It was cool now, and she gulped the tasty liquid. Lot had left his empty bowl on the ground. She picked it up and went back around the tent.

As she went about her work that day, Hagar reflected on her strange experience with Lot. He had sought her out, then quizzed her about her final words with Terah. Why? What was he trying to find out?

She wondered what Lot had been about to say before Sarai interrupted him. Maybe . . . maybe . . . if she had talked with him some more, she might have learned what her ultimate purpose was in the family of Abram.

5

The day after Terah's death, Abram announced his decision to move to the west.

The thirty days of mourning became a bustle of activity as the tribe prepared for the journey. The sheep were sheared and the barley harvested. Sacks of grain occupied space in every tent, waiting to be packed onto the backs of donkeys. Sheep, goats, and grain, mused Hagar. They would provide meat, milk and bread for the long journey.

Like everyone else, Hagar threw herself into the preparations. She was so busy she had no time to ask questions about her mysterious place in the family. The few times she had an opportunity to ask Sarai, she was given a mumbled "Later," and turned away. Lot was busy with his own preparations for the journey, but Hagar did not want to ask him anyway. The less she saw of him, the better.

Only half the clan would be moving. Abram's family had continued living in tents, while Nahor's tribe had built the more permanent mud and brick cone-shaped houses. Who would go and who would stay had been settled long ago. Hagar was disappointed that Lot would go with Abram.

Hagar, like all the slaves, walked. Her mistress Sarai rode a donkey. At first the procession was cheerful, and laughter often heard.

Abram had planned well. The long procession stretched out for almost a mile, with several hundred men scattered among the herds and flocks. The pace was set for the slowest animals. Behind them the guards made sure there were no stragglers.

Several times, Hagar spotted roving groups of men on the horizon. "Amurru," said Sarai in answer to her question. "I wish they'd stay on their side of the river. They're looking for stragglers."

Hagar shuddered, thankful for the many armed men who surrounded the clan.

They met a few caravans, their donkeys loaded with trade goods, destined for the markets in the big cities of the "Between Rivers" plain. Slave caravans were not uncommon. As they passed, Hagar was struck by the contrast between the slaves' sullen faces and slumped shoulders — and the cheerful demeanor and proud carriage of the servants and slaves of Abram's clan.

As the day wore on, Hagar grew weary, but she plodded on. She carried a bundle of household goods and a goatskin filled with water. The skin emptied quickly, as men, women, and children came to her for a drink. She was careful to refill the goatskin at every stream they crossed.

By the time they arrived at their first campsite, she was exhausted. So, it seemed, was everyone else. They built no cooking fires, and everyone seemed glad to eat the small cakes of unleavened bread they had packed. They chewed dried meat and washed it down with water. The livestock were milked, then everyone rolled into a blanket and slept on the ground. Everyone, that is, except the first watch, who struggled to keep awake through the early hours of the night.

Hagar at first dropped into a deep sleep, but she was awakened by sharp pains in her legs. Cramps! Muscles unused to such strenuous activity protested loudly. Not only her legs — her back, stomach, sides and shoulders ached. She tossed and turned, gasping, whimpering, often standing to straighten her muscles. She tried to do it softly, but Sarai wakened and noticed her discomfort.

When morning came, Hagar could hardly walk. But she knew she would have to. Eventually the aches in her muscles would ease.

"Ride my donkey," commanded Sarai.

Hagar gratefully obeyed. She had never ridden a donkey for a long time before, and she was unprepared for the discomfort. She soon mastered the art of riding, using a small crop to guide the gentle, well-trained beast. But even though she rode side-saddle, the sharp backbone cut into her body. Before an hour had passed, she was acutely aware of the sharpness of the animal's back.

"Mother Sarai," she gasped. "Please. May I walk a while?"

Sarai laughed, and they exchanged places. Walking was easier than riding the sharp-backed donkey, especially after she had walked enough that her muscle pains eased.

An hour later, Sarai said, "Your turn again!" and slid off the donkey to help Hagar mount. And so it continued throughout that day and the next, taking turns.

Progress was slow. From Haran to Carchemish, where they would cross the Euphrates River, they plodded along the ancient caravan route. On a fast donkey, the trip would take two or three days. With a large clan migration, it took twelve. They arrived in the country of the Amurru late in the dry season, the hottest time of the year.

Abram, with his usual efficiency, had sent messengers ahead to the Amurru in Carchemish, along with gifts and assurances of peace. Several days passed there while they crossed the river. Hagar was grateful for the inflated goatskins which kept her afloat as she struggled across the deepest part of the river. The animals had to swim.

Here they settled into a semipermanent camp. The slaves gathered the dried sheep dung for fires. For the first time since they left Haran, they cooked food. Soon the campsite was filled with savory odors from the cooking pots. After a dozen days of cold food, the mutton stew and fresh barley bread were welcome.

The Amurru came out of their walled city to trade with them. The travelers added to their diet by buying their figs, honey, nuts, olives, and even a crude wine. The wine was better than the water of the river, constantly muddied by the animals.

The Amurru people, seemingly delighted at the profit made by selling food to these strangers, were obviously uncomfortable with so large a clan encamped outside

Carchemish. The sheep and goats cleaned out all the good pasture land, and at this time of the year there was little to begin with. Abram assured the Amurru he too was eager to move on. He wanted to arrive at Aleppo before the *yoreh*, when the winter rains began and the roads became impassible. After a few days rest at Carchemish, the procession continued.

Their caravan route led directly to the two great population centers — Aleppo and Ebla. Even though it followed a much-traveled route, the road was rugged. It took them through many wadis, over mountain passes, across grassless steppes. When they finally arrived in the fertile Chalys River valley where Aleppo dominated the plain, they were exhausted. Abram decreed a semi-permanent stop for the five months of the rainy season.

Abram pitched his tents to the south of Aleppo, half way between that city and Ebla. The King's Highway passed through there, and Abram declared that from here on the going would be easier. Nevertheless, he wanted to stay for the rainy season. They could plant their barley crops. When they harvested it after the *malkosh*, the last rain of the year, they would have enough grain to keep them supplied for the rest of the journey.

On the day after their arrival they were milking the livestock in the early morning. Just then the king of Aleppo came out to greet the strangers encamped so near his city.

Abram planned to stand alone by the river to greet the king. He had told his people to continue with the milking. However, a large crowd of his family and servants gathered at the riverside to watch. Hagar, being a *shifkhah*, a slave with special privileges, was not involved in the milking. She stood beside Sarai and saw and heard everything.

"Greetings, great king of Aleppo," said Abram heartily. "May God give you a good day."

The king came to a stop about ten paces in front of Abram. Behind him ranged his small retinue of men.

"Thank you for your gift," he said curtly, referring to the gifts Abram had sent him in advance.

Hagar was accustomed to men who wore their hair combed and oiled, their beards neatly trimmed. This man, with his shaggy beard and hair, looked almost barbarian. Yet his linen robe was clean, cut in the eastern style, and trimmed in many colors. The men behind him, however, wore ragged skins.

Hagar noticed something else about the

men. They leaned on their spears, their eyes listless. They seemed to totter, as though sick.

Abram had been carefully observing them also. "Is all well in your city?" he asked in a soothing voice.

The king frowned, glaring at him beneath shaggy brows. "Everything is as it should be!" he barked.

Abram smiled. "We have just milked our animals. May we share some of this milk with you now?"

The king continued to glower at Abram. Finally he growled, "At what price?"

Abram shook his head. "No price. A gift." He turned to the people behind him. "Bring milk for our guests."

Hagar hurried to obey him. She filled an empty goatskin water bag with fresh milk and brought it to the king. He lifted the bag to his mouth and held it high while he drank greedily, the white liquid running down his beard. Hagar was glad she had filled the bag.

When at last he finished, Hagar handed the bag to the men behind the king. They too drank as though they were drinking the finest wine. There was no sound except the loud slurping of the men as they drank.

"Thank you," muttered the king. He still glared at Abram, his eyes hostile. "How long will you stay?"

Hagar suddenly realized why the king was so unfriendly. He was afraid of Abram and his clan. He wanted them to move on as quickly as possible. But why? Was it because the people of Aleppo were sick and could not defend themselves?

When Abram spoke, his voice was friendly. "Great king, we plan to be here through the rainy season. We mean you no harm, and we will leave following the *malkosh,* the last rain."

Abram paused, gazing steadily at the king. When he spoke, his words were slow. "During the rainy season, we will send in to the city a portion of our daily milk supply."

The king's head jerked up. He opened his mouth, closed it, swallowed, and finally spoke.

"Why do you do this? What price are you asking?"

"No price." Again Abram smiled, keeping his voice soothing. "This is a gift of friendship and good will. Let us say it is in payment for the privilege of remaining in your country for a few months."

The king continued to glower at Abram, perhaps searching his face for signs of perfidy. Finally he nodded. "I accept your gift," he said curtly. "Thank you."

He turned abruptly and with his men

walked quickly toward the city gates.

Abram turned sharply to his people, but his chuckle softened his words. "What are you all doing here, standing around? There's work to be done! If we're going to stay here a while, let's be sure we have decent tents to live in!"

His words were greeted with a burst of laughter stirred by nervous relief. They scattered to their various jobs.

Later Hagar learned that the people of Aleppo were indeed sick. A plague had wiped out their livestock. All they owned were the few sheep, goats, and asses Abram had sent as his advance gift. Lacking an adequate supply of milk and meat, the people were starving. Abram's gift of daily milk had perhaps saved them from extinction.

6

The city gates of Aleppo were solid but vulnerable. Made of wood, they could be burned or battered down if the attacker were determined enough. They were closed now. The defenders undoubtedly felt they faced a dangerous enemy in the migrating clan camped two miles away on the banks of the Chalys River — the clan that had sent fresh milk for the past five months to help the city survive.

Hagar gazed thoughtfully at the city, thinking about its closed gates. Why was the king so sullen, although the townspeople were friendly and seemingly grateful? Often they had come out of the city to trade, sometimes to give gifts, although lately they had been whispering and casting furtive glances in the direction of Abram's tents.

But the king never came out. To Hagar, he seemed to sulk and brood behind his closed gates.

Why? Was he an ungrateful boor, who accepted lifegiving gifts with resentment? Was he so proud he could not accept a gift so precious, and gratitude turned to gall in his stomach? If so, what would he do about it?

The people of Aleppo grew stronger every day. Those who came out of the city to mingle with Abram's clan were now robust and healthy, thanks to the daily supply of milk. Surely the king could see the benefits of Abram's generosity. Why would he act so hostile?

Five months ago, the only time the king had come out to meet Abram, he had seemed to fear the clan. That could be explained by the weakness of the people — they were vulnerable to attack. Maybe it had happened before. That would certainly make any king hesitant to offer the hand of friendship to a foreign invader. Maybe that weakness had been the only thing keeping the king from attacking Abram. But now, now that they were strong again, what was there to keep him from —

Hagar gasped as the frightening thought struck her. She looked again at the city gates. She pictured a horde of Amurru pouring out, heavily armed, attacking the peaceful clan encamped on the riverbank. While everyone slept. Slaughter. Bloodshed. Screams. Death.

She shuddered and hurried back to Abram's tent.

Sarai was coming out, carrying a small bag of barley to be ground into meal for bread. She glanced sharply at Hagar.

"What's the matter, child? Did you see something that frightened you?"

Hagar stopped, trying to compose herself. Should she tell her mistress her fears? Or were they just the imaginings of a silly girl? Would Mother Sarai laugh at her? Maybe. But it might be better to be laughed at now than murdered in the middle of the night.

"Mother Sarai. . . ." She paused, not knowing what to say.

Sarai smiled. "Tell me, Hagar. What's troubling you?"

Hagar took a deep breath and blurted, "What would happen if that king of Aleppo suddenly took it into his head to come out and attack us? Like in the middle of the night. Do you think — ?"

Sarai laughed, but the laugh was not derisive. Hagar pressed her point.

"Please, Mother Sarai. Maybe I'm being silly, but I've been wondering why the king was so mad at us. Maybe he sees in us a threat to attack him."

"But child, we give him milk. We've helped his city. Why would he — "

Sarai didn't finish. Instead she turned and looked thoughtfully at the city in the distance.

Hagar said nothing. She had sown the seed; now she let it grow. Finally Sarai turned back. She frowned.

"I'll tell Abram," she said.

Hagar did not overhear Sarai's conversation with Abram but saw Abram post guards on the city side of the camp that night. He seemed less cheerful during the next three days. Several times Hagar caught him staring at her.

As the days passed, Hagar noticed a tension developing in Abram. He posted more guards at night, scattering them around the camp. Something of his worry must have been communicated, for often the people of the clan cast anxious looks at the city.

The citizens of Aleppo who came out to trade with them had been cheerful and friendly. But Hagar noticed a change. They were now hesitant and sullen. Perhaps they too felt the tension from inside the city. In their gratitude they seemed to be trying to warn Abram and his clan. But no one would speak openly, perhaps out of fear.

The *malkosh*, the last rain of the season, was not far off. The rainy season in this part of the country was not as long and as severe as they had anticipated. Maybe it was over and the dry season was already upon them. In this dry weather, the barley would ripen quickly and could be harvested. Then they could move on.

Hagar noticed that Abram also scanned the skies, probably wondering if the *malkosh* had already occurred.

"Tomorrow," he declared, "we will harvest the barley. It will be ripe enough. But today we will prepare to move. We must pack supplies we laid out during our stay and prepare to travel."

All during that day, Hagar was aware that no visitors came to the camp from the city. That night she went to bed with a very uneasy feeling. She slept in Abram's broad tent, now filled with that familiar organized clutter of a family ready to move. She had trouble falling asleep, and slept lightly.

She awakened sometime during the night, when a voice at the tent flap called, "Father Abram!"

Abram was immediately on his feet. "What is it, Mardi?"

Hagar could not see the man, who remained outside the tent. As Abram lifted the flap and went out, she heard Mardi's whispered, "There's someone here, from the city. He says. . . ."

She couldn't hear the rest, but she guessed what the visitor would have to say.

A few moments later, Abram stuck his head in the door of the tent.

"Everyone up!" he said softly, but Hagar sensed the tension in his voice. "God has spoken. We are moving. Now. Before dawn!"

Then he left to warn the rest of the camp. Hagar heard his commands, even though couched in a soft voice. "Up! Up! Everyone. We're moving. God has spoken to me. We will be attacked today by the king of Aleppo. We must be away from here as soon as possible!"

God has spoken? Hagar shook her head in awe. Had he really? No. The warning had come from one of the citizens of Aleppo. Hadn't it?

The clan immediately went into an organized turmoil. Sarai stood just outside the tent, giving orders to her slaves to complete the packing The tents were disassembled and bundled into small enough packages to fit on the donkeys. All the packs which had been so carefully prepared during the past few days were now placed on the waiting beasts. The people moved quietly and with practiced efficiency, sensing the threat which hung over them.

Before dawn, they were on their way.

Traveling south along the King's Highway

was considerably easier than traveling from Haran to Aleppo. Even in the pre-dawn darkness, they had no trouble following the broad caravan trail along the face of the mountain range which rose steeply to the right. Soon they passed the ancient, sprawling city of Ebla, just starting to come alive in the new day.

Hagar walked, while Sarai rode. They followed the pattern established earlier, taking turns.

Suddenly Abram appeared beside her as she walked. In the early dawn, his hair and beard seemed strangely ruffled. He had not taken the time to oil and comb them as he usually did each morning.

"Hagar," he said, speaking slowly. "What will happen now do you think? Will they follow and attack us?"

Hagar caught her breath and wrinkled her brow. Why ask her? She didn't know anything about such things. She was only a young slave girl. Abram was the one God was supposed to speak to. Why should he question her about such things?

"I . . . I don't know, sir."

"Tell me, child. What do you think? Surely you have some ideas."

Hagar swallowed, then took a deep breath. She would have to say something.

But what? What was she expected to say?

"Well, maybe — maybe the king won't follow. Maybe when he sees that we've gone — " Was she saying the right things? She hoped so.

She stumbled on. "Maybe when he sees that we left behind the barley unharvested he won't . . . oh, I don't know. Do you think — ?"

Abram shrugged. "Maybe so. Yes. The barley harvest. He would reap that for himself. That may be our salvation. God has delivered us again."

Abruptly he turned and trudged back along the column.

Hagar glanced at her mistress, riding beside her. Sarai was close enough that she had heard everything.

"Mother Sarai, I don't understand. Why did he ask me? I don't know anything about that sort of thing."

Sarai was silent for a moment before replying. "I don't know, child. Maybe he respects your opinion. After all, it *was* you who warned him about the king."

"Yes, but — "

"Never mind, Hagar. Who knows what Abram is thinking? I still don't understand him, and I've been married to him for a good many years!"

7

"Good morning, Hagar. Is everything all right with you?"

Abram's voice startled her as she walked. The clan was migrating southward on the King's Highway. Abram walked beside her, matching his stride to hers. They plodded along at a slow pace, the same speed as the slowest of the flocks.

Abram's question did not surprise her. She had heard him ask it before, many times, since they left Aleppo several months ago. Hagar had been aware of Abram's concern for all the people of his clan, and he often asked everyone the same question. He listened carefully to their answers.

Hagar could not stifle the laugh which bubbled out. "Yes, Father Abram. On a day such as this, everything's very right!"

She breathed deeply of the early morning air. The oppressive heat which would soon descend on them had not yet flushed from the air the humidity left over from the night. The newly risen sun glistened on the snow-capped peak in the west. She marveled again that there was snow there at this time of the year, just before the *yoreh,* the first rain. Overhead, a flock of storks glided southward in search of a winter home.

Abram smiled, obviously delighted at her youthful exuberance. "Yes, another beautiful day, given to us by the generous hand of our God. But soon we must think about stopping for the rainy season. We must plant another crop, which this time we must harvest for ourselves."

Abram's smile disappeared, and he looked solemnly at Hagar. "Tell me, my dear, do you think we ought to push on toward Hazor, or stay on the King's Highway until we reach the Sea of Chinnereth?"

Hagar shook her head, and her voice reflected her amusement. "How should I know, Father Abram? Am I to make all your decisions for you?"

Abram laughed, as Hagar knew he would. Since she had come to live with this clan, she had learned to be comfortable in the presence of the patriarch. He never rebuked her for this kind of familiarity, and he always laughed when she gently teased him. She had told Sarai several times that Abram was more a father than a master to her.

By now she was also used to his looking to her for help with decisions. She had discussed this with Sarai. They concluded Abram believed that somehow God spoke to him through Hagar. At first it had puzzled her, but with Sarai's help, she now found it only amusing. Yet she knew Abram took it seriously.

Her familiarity with Abram led her to believe she could confront him with the question she and Sarai had often discussed. She turned to him now.

"Father Abram, may I ask you something?"

Her serious tone must have startled him, for he glanced at her, frowning. "Of course, my child. Ask whatever you like."

He was so unlike what a master should be! Somehow calling him "Father Abram" seemed appropriate.

"I would like to know why you think I would know about such things as where you should spend the rainy season. Do you think God speaks to you through me?"

She was startled by her own boldness. She almost wished she had not asked. Had she gone too far?

But Abram's frown disappeared, and his good humor reasserted itself. "God speaks in many ways, my child. He never speaks to me in an audible voice, as I am speaking to you right now. But he does speak. He speaks to me through that flock of storks passing overhead, telling me the *yoreh* is near.

"He speaks to me through the messenger who came last night, telling me that the king of Hazor was unfriendly, in spite of my gifts to him. He speaks to me through Sarai, who tells me how tired some of our people are, that we must stop soon."

"But sir, is this truly God speaking to you? Or is it just your good sense trying to make a decision?"

Now she knew she had gone too far. But Abram only turned to her and smiled gently.

"My dear, when you open yourself to listen to the voice of God, you can hear him plainly. Some day you too will hear him. I feel sure of that."

"Me? But I don't even believe in your God. I was raised to be a follower of Yarah. Your God would never speak to me."

"You don't believe in that moon goddess any more than I do. Just wait. Some day our God will speak to you, and then you will know," Abram retorted.

"Well, maybe so, but he hasn't spoken to me this morning — at least, not yet!"

Again she wondered if her flippancy

would offend him. But he only laughed.

"My child, you have so much to learn. He *does* speak through you. Didn't he warn me through you that the king of Aleppo would attack us? Didn't he tell me through you that the wicked king would take our barley harvest and not follow us? Of course God speaks through you, even if you don't hear his voice."

Hagar pulled the cowl of her robe around her head, to protect her from sun as it beat on the left side of her face. Already the morning had lost its pleasantness; soon the heat would be oppressive.

Father Abram's religious views were far beyond anything she could understand. But she did not despise his way of looking at things. She envied him, she realized. If only she could have faith like that!

"Father Abram, do you know where we're going? Has God told you yet where the land he will give you is?"

"Not yet, child. But he will. I'm sure of it." He turned to her, chuckling. "Maybe he'll tell me through you. For all we know, you might be leading us into Egypt!"

Hagar wondered how Abram could speak of such important matters so lightheartedly. But that was Abram's way. His thoughts were serious and profound, even if his words were frivolous and surrounded with laughter.

His good humor was infectious. She too laughed. "In that case, why don't I lead you to my father's old farm?"

"Where was that, Hagar?"

"I'm not sure. Somewhere in Lower Egypt, in the Delta. But then, maybe God will show you exactly where it is."

He nodded, but he did not smile at this. His next words were sober. "Yes," he said softly. "Maybe he will."

"Hagar! Slow down!" Sarai's voice came to them from behind. "Wait for me."

Both Abram and Hagar stopped and turned to watch Sarai urge her small donkey forward. When she finally caught up with them, she lightly slid off its back and began walking. The donkey followed with no urging.

"Your turn to ride, Hagar," said Sarai, rubbing her back. "God created that beast with a knife blade under its skin."

Hagar laughed. "I'm not ready to ride yet, Mother Sarai. It's too much fun walking."

As the days had passed, she had grown accustomed to long hours of trudging slowly south along the King's Highway. Each day she spent less time on the donkey.

"How are you, my dear?"

Abram's voice reflected his love for his

wife. Although Hagar had been with them for a year, she still marveled at the close affection between these two. She was used to marriages of conveniences, where the husband cared nothing for his wife except as a way of siring his heirs.

"Very well," replied Sarai, "as soon as I can get that donkey's sword out of my back."

"It's the donkey I feel sorry for." Abram eyed the small beast reflectively. "He has that knife in his back all the time!"

"What do you think, husband," said Sarai. "Should we take turns carrying the donkey?"

As Hagar joined their laughter, she tried to remember when she had last heard a family display so much good humor. She decided she had never seen anything like it. Not even her parents were like that. She recalled them as somber people, too concerned about crops and tools and beasts of burden to indulge in such frivolity as laughter.

"Father Abram! Wait!"

Hagar turned at the sound of the urgent voice behind them. Lot was running toward them, the skirts of his robe high. The awkward fifteen-year-old boy held up his long shepherd's staff to keep from tripping over it, making him look like a very young lamb frisking on a hillside.

In spite of the urgency of Lot's approach, Hagar smiled. What was it this time? Everything he did or said was so important! One of his sheep was limping. A goat was about to give birth. A donkey's eyes were red and watery. A burr had stuck in his hair. Life and death matters. What was it now? Had he broken one of his fingernails?

"Father Abram!" He pulled up, panting, in front of the patriarch. "Mardi! He says come quick! The Canaanites!"

"Slow down, boy." Abram's voice was calm. He knew about Lot's tendency to get excited over little things. "Now tell me about the Canaanites? What do they want?"

"Want! They want to kill us all and take our flocks, that's what they want! They're going to attack us! You'd better come quick, and bring some of your men!"

"How do you know they want to attack? Maybe they just want to trade. Or bring messages from the king of Hazor. What makes you think they want to fight?"

"They're armed! They — they just stand there and watch us. Like they're waiting for their chance."

"All right. I'd better come." Abram turned to Sarai and Hagar. "Don't be alarmed. It's probably nothing serious."

"Nothing serious!" Lot's voice was louder than respect permitted. "You call a bunch of Canaanites ready to attack nothing serious?"

Most clan leaders would be offended by this disrespect. But Hagar had been aware of Abram's indulgence of his nephew. Abram made allowances for outbursts that would normally have called for a beating.

Abram put his arm around Lot's shoulder and walked off with him. Hagar could hear him speaking to his nephew, his words placating and comforting, assuring him there was no danger.

"What do you think, Mother Sarai?" Hagar turned and walked beside her mistress as they resumed their journey. "Is it serious? Or is Lot just making a major war out of a little group of friendly Canaanites?"

Sarai chuckled. "I think Lot's too full of his own importance. Has he been bothering you lately?"

Hagar hesitated. "No . . . nothing I can't handle."

Sarai noticed her hesitation. "That boy!" She shook her head in disgust. "What he needs is a wife."

"I hope he doesn't want me."

Hagar had been aware of the young man's

persistent attention to her through the past year. She had tried to avoid him, but the youth seized every opportunity to speak to her. She found this offensive, but she could not understand why. Something about his attitude toward her. The way he looked at her. His arrogance. Even the way he spoke her name. And he was the only one in Abram's household who made her feel that way.

Sarai's next words surprised her. "He has asked for you, as a matter of fact."

"Me? He wants me to be his wife?"

"No. Not his wife. His concubine."

Hagar trudged beside her mistress while she thought about that. Of course, he had every right. She was a slave, and it was not proper to think of herself as worthy of a wife's place. But a concubine had no rights or privileges as a wife had. Her children would be the children of the wife, not her own. She did not want to be Lot's concubine.

Nor his wife, for that matter.

She turned to Sarai. "Did he ask Father Abram for me?"

"Yes."

"And what did Father Abram say?"

Sarai smiled grimly. "He said no. Emphatically. In fact, he told Lot that you would eventually be a wife, not a concubine, and you would have to approve before he would make any arrangements."

"Father Abram said that?"

Sarai nodded. "Not only that. He asked me what I thought about it. I told him you would never consent to marrying Lot. And I wouldn't permit it. Not you."

"What . . . what do you plan to do with me?"

Sarai was silent for a moment before replying. When she finally spoke, her words were soft. "You'll know in due time. But meanwhile — " She turned to Hagar and flashed a broad smile. "We ought to do something about finding Lot a wife to keep him busy."

That made a lot of sense to Hagar. Lot was a lusty young man. She wasn't sure how she knew that, but she was sure of it. He needed to have someone to . . . well, divert his attention from her.

"Does Abram have anyone in mind for Lot?"

"No. Not yet. Other than yourself, there are only two girls among our servants who are of the right age. But they are daughters of slaves. And Abram doesn't want to marry him to a Canaanite or some other foreigner."

"Why not? Couldn't he make an alliance with some king and get Lot a princess? That would take care of several different things at once."

"Hmm. A princess. I never would have thought of that. Yes. Yes, I'll suggest that to Abram. See what he thinks."

"Will you tell him it's my suggestion?"

"Of course." Sarai nodded and smiled. "I see. You want him to know you don't want Lot for yourself. Is that it?"

"Yes, Mother Sarai."

But that was not it. Not it at all.

What she really wanted was that Abram accept it as God's will. God, speaking through the slave girl, Hagar, saying to the clan patriarch that Lot should be married to a Canaanite princess. Abram would probably do it. God's will. God's voice speaking to him — through her!

Something stirred inside Hagar. Something deep, only vaguely understood. Here was a means of doing things she had never dreamed of doing. Controlling her master. Getting him to do what she wanted.

She shivered, in spite of the day's oppressive heat. The feeling of power was delicious. And dangerous. She didn't know whether she liked it or not.

8

Abram decided not to spend the winter encamped by the city of Hazor. Or rather, Hagar thought wryly, God told him not to.

Abram seemed to hurry their pace as they trudged southward on the King's Highway. Their route took them to the east of the vast Sea of Chinnereth, where Hagar could see the white sails of fishing boats on the bright blue water. Would Abram continue on the King's Highway all the way to the Salt Sea, or would he go west to the Great Sea and take the coastal road to Egypt? Hagar wondered what God would say to Abram about that.

The *yoreh* was imminent. The dry season had run its course, and the land seemed parched. Clouds gathered in the sky, threatening to open and soak the travelers any day. The flocks and herds were weary. They needed to stop soon for the rainy season.

But Abram pressed on.

Fortunately the King's Highway was easy to follow. There were no rugged peaks to scale, no rushing streams to cross, and enough inhabitants to trade with. Often Abram was able to trade a few goats for some sacks of wheat or barley, which provided them with bread. Having missed the harvest of their own barley crop, they were in dire need of these grains.

The one thing the King's Highway did not provide was an adequate supply of pasture land for the sheep and goats. Sooner or later they must descend to the Jordan Valley to the west, where the flocks would find pasturage.

When they came to the Yarmuk River, Hagar was sure Abram would turn westward, following it down into the Jordan valley just south of the Sea of Chinnereth. Instead he continued on the King's Highway to the south. He gave no indication of his reasons.

They crossed the Arab River, just a trickle in this late season. At the Yabis River, they had another opportunity to descend into the Jordan valley, but again Abram continued on the King's Highway. They made their way down to the fords of the Jabbok River. There Abram finally made his decision. He turned west, away from the King's Highway to the broad valley floor of the Jordan River.

Still the *yoreh* did not come. Hagar wondered, as she looked around this marshy, reed-grown flatland, if a major rainstorm would swell the Jordan River and wash them away. But at least there was pasturage here.

There were also thickets so dense and impenetrable that the sheep and goats could only nibble on the edges. What wild animals lurked there? Hagar had heard stories about bears and lions and other monsters which inhabited this dark valley and preyed on unwary travelers. She shuddered and vowed she would stay close to camp.

As they prepared for their first night, Hagar and Sarai lit cooking fires while the servants erected the tents. The fire, made of sheep chips, burned well. Soon a goat was roasting on the spit. From the small city of Adam, built on a promontory above the Jordan River, they had obtained some wheat. They would bake bread in the coals to complement the meat at the evening meal.

Hagar and Sarai were startled by a loud flapping noise. They looked up to see a large flock of storks descending on the valley. The birds flew into a grove of tamarisk trees, taking about an hour to noisily settle for the night. As the sun set, the trees seemed to blossom white with the roosting birds.

Abram stood in front of the grove of trees, feet spread apart, hands behind his back, beard pointed toward the trees. The picture of a man in deep concentration. Hagar suppressed a giggle. Was God speaking to him through those storks?

"Abram," called Sarai. "Come and eat. Those storks are taking care of themselves. *We* need to take care of us!"

Abram sighed as he approached the fire and sat on a log. He accepted gratefully a bowl of meat and a hunk of bread. Sarai had thoughtfully spread some goat grease on the bread for flavor.

"Father Abram." Hagar sank down on a flat rock beside him, assuming the now familiar role of daughter. "Do you plan to stay here for the winter? There is good pasturage."

"I don't know, child." Abram wiped some grease from his beard. "I don't think it would be wise to stay here long. The valley will flood after the *yoreh*."

"Then we're going up into the mountains to the west?"

Abram nodded. "There is a good valley just north of here. It takes us up to a high country, where the flocks can have plenty of water and good grazing, and we can plant our crops for the rainy season."

Sarai joined them with her own bowl of meat and bread. "But couldn't we stay here for a while? Our people need rest. And the sheep and goats surely need to graze on this rich Jordan grass."

Abram nodded. "You're right, my dear. We're all tired of traveling."

Hagar looked over across the reeds where the Jordan River curved like a writhing snake through the broad valley. She wondered if God would speak to Abram through his weariness and tell him to stop here. But if God were smart, he would know whether the Jordan River would flood and wash them away.

She bit her lip. She shouldn't be so flippant. Maybe Abram's God really did exist, and spoke to Abram just like he said. If so, then was she blaspheming in thinking this way?

"Father Abram," she said shyly, trying to cover up her own boldness. "What would happen if God caused a big rainfall in the mountains back there?" She waved vaguely in the direction of the towering ridges to the east, from which they had descended."What if all the rain would pour down the streams and into this valley? Wouldn't we all be swept away?"

"Yes, Hagar." Abram's tone was almost condescending. "That's why we can't stay here. This is not a good campground, for that very reason. But we might be safe for a few days."

"But . . . Father Abram. Please don't think I'm too forward, but. . . ." She looked at her bowl, now empty. Then she sighed, and continued softly. "Shouldn't we — well, be on the other side of the river now? What if the *yoreh* would come tonight? Wouldn't we all drown?"

Sarai's gentle laugh reached her. "Oh, Hagar. Don't worry. Nothing like that will happen."

But Abram didn't laugh. He regarded his adopted daughter soberly, a frown playing upon his forehead. "Why do you say that, my dear?" he asked.

"I don't know." Hagar wouldn't look at him. "I can just picture the flood here, and the sheep getting caught with their wool soaked, and the goats — " She shuddered. "It can't happen, can it?"

Again Sarai laughed, but before she could say anything, Abram spoke in a somber voice. "We'll move tomorrow," he said.

Sarai's laugh dried up and she turned to her husband. "Tomorrow? But what about our rest? What about the sheep and goats grazing for a while? We're so tired!"

"Nevertheless — " Abram paused and took a deep breath. "We move on tomorrow morning. Hagar may be right."

Hagar, her eyes on her empty bowl, felt Sarai's stare. It seemed to bore into her, penetrating the deepest secret caverns of her thoughts. Did her mistress guess her schemes and plots? Or was she impressed, like her husband, that somehow God spoke to Abram through her?

She must be careful. Sarai must not know. Sarai must not be given any clue to guess what she planned. She must not suspect that her innocent suggestion had been planted in Abram's mind as a test of her ability to manipulate him.

It had almost been too obvious tonight. Hagar bit her lip. She would have to be more careful.

9

The *yoreh,* the first rain of the season, began to fall as they were fording the Jordan River.

Hagar, on foot and burdened by a pack and water bag, looked at the stream fearfully. At this end of the dry season, the waters of the Jordan came a little above her knees, although the current was strong. How much time did they have before this rain turned it into a raging, swirling torrent? Maybe God really had spoken through her last night. Was it raining in the mountains to the north? And how long would it take for runoff to reach this ford? Hagar shuddered. She pressed on toward the other side.

The rain was light and did not last long. Before noon, the entire entourage had crossed, and Abram led them westward across the wide, flat country. In a few hours they came to another river, which Abram called the Fayad. They crossed this, too, and set up camp in the broad valley.

Tents were assembled and fires lit. By now, all knew their responsibilities and the camp was soon ready for the night. The stew cooking in the pot contained little besides meat. They were almost out of grain.

Sarai looked around at the servants moving listlessly about their duties. She sighed.

"We'll have to stop soon," she said to Hagar. "Everybody's tired. The livestock too. And we need to plant a barley crop."

Hagar had sensed the exhaustion of the clan and the animals. There was plenty of meat for the stewpots, since more and more of the sheep and goats were dying every day. When they left Haran, the clan of Abram had been the wealthiest family in the country, even after the division of property following Terah's death. Now, although a large number of livestock remained, they risked losing all.

"Mother Sarai," she said shyly. "Is this a good place to stop for the rainy season?"

"What do you mean, Hagar? Look around you. Broad valley, lots of grass, fertile land for our grain fields, fresh water — what more could you ask?"

"Does this area flood during the rainy season?"

Sarai frowned. "I don't know. But Abram should. He talks to all the local people. We're going to have to stop somewhere."

"Yes, Mother Sarai."

Hagar became aware of Sarai's gaze upon her. She sensed something in her mistress — a calculation, a bewildered appraisal, a deep probe into Hagar's thoughts. What was she thinking? She didn't have long to wait.

"Hagar." Sarai's voice was low, thoughtful. "Why don't you speak to Abram? Tell him we must stop soon."

"Me? Will he listen to me?"

Sarai nodded. "He will. You know how he respects your . . . opinion."

Hagar stared at her feet. Sarai knew, then! She suspected — or knew — about Hagar's ability to manipulate Abram by pretending God spoke to him through her. But to ask her to use this power of manipulation — Sarai couldn't be too angry with her about it. Maybe she thought if she could control Hagar, then she could control Abram — through Hagar!

"I'll try, Mother Sarai." Hagar spoke softly. "But I still don't think my opinion is important."

Sarai's voice was sharper than she had ever heard it before. "Yes it is, Hagar. You know it. And I think you'd better speak to him tonight."

"Yes, my lady."

"Good." Sarai glanced over toward the river, where she could see Abram coming toward them in the early darkness. "Here he comes now. Don't forget!"

"Yes, my lady."

Hagar hurried to ladle some stew into a bowl for Abram as he approached. As she handed it to him, she noticed the lines of worry on his forehead. His smile of thanks was brief. With a sigh he sank down on the carpet to eat.

"Everything is quiet for the night," he muttered between mouthfuls. "But we'll move on in the morning."

Sarai, seated beside him, shot a dark glance at Hagar. The slave girl sat on the carpet beside them, knowing she would have to say something but not sure how to begin.

"Father Abram." Her voice was small, and her eyes were on the ground.

"Yes, my child?" When Hagar didn't reply instantly, he went on. "I shouldn't be calling you a child any longer. You're growing up. And what a beautiful young lady you are becoming!"

"Thank you, Father Abram." She looked up and smiled tentatively, then looked away again. "I was wondering — I mean — "

"Yes, young lady? Go ahead. Speak. You know it's all right."

"Yes, Father Abram." She took a deep breath, aware of Sarai's gaze upon her. "I was wondering . . . about when we are going to stop for the rainy season. Shouldn't we pretty soon — "

"Yes, Hagar." Abram did not seem angry that his slave girl would speak to him that way. But then he never had before. "I know what you're thinking. Sarai has talked about this a lot too. The people are tired. The animals are exhausted and starving. We have no grain left, and must put in a barley crop soon. I know all the problems." He sighed. "I'm waiting for God to tell me what to do."

"Couldn't we just stay here?"

"No, Hagar." Abram glanced at Sarai, and a small smile played on his face. "I sense a conspiracy here. Tell me, wife, did you put her up to this?"

To Hagar's surprise, Sarai nodded. "Yes, husband. I know you respect her opinion. Sometimes God speaks to you through her. Isn't it about time you listen?"

Hagar had been aware of the honesty which passed between her master and mistress ever since joining their household more than a year before. She had been pleased, because she too had always practiced total honesty and candor in her relationships with her owners. She wondered how much

Abram suspected of the real conspiracy behind Hagar's simple question.

Abram's answer was thoughtfully phrased. "I *have* been listening to the voice of God. He speaks to me through the condition of the herds and flocks, and the tiredness of my people. He speaks to me through the need for more grain, which I can't buy from the inhabitants of this poor country.

"But God also speaks to me through the season. I know that soon this valley will be flooded. It is not a good place to be caught in a downpour, or when the heavy rains come to the uplands around us. The torrent will carry away our sheep, and wash away our crops.

"In this way God tells me to move on. The sooner the better."

Hagar turned her face toward the darkness so Abram could not see her smile. The seed she had planted *had* borne fruit! She was aware of Abram's way of saying that God spoke to him when actually his good sense and thoughtful appraisal of the situation had spoken. A deeply religious person would undoubtedly see things that way.

It seemed strange to her, but only because she didn't believe in the invisible God Abram claimed was all around her. But if that was what Abram believed, she would accept it. As long as he continued to make his decisions using his own common sense and knowledge, he could call it anything he wanted.

Why, then, did he believe God sometimes spoke through her?

Sarai's voice interrupted her thoughts. "Where *do* you plan to stop for the season, my husband?"

"Shechem, I suppose." Abram laid down his now empty bowl. "It's not far from here, on the upper plateau. We'll be there in a few days. Maybe God will speak to me there."

Hagar felt the need to ask an important question. She knew Shechem was a small town in the hill country ahead; Abram had spoken of it before. A caravan crossroad. The town was small, but the location was important.

"Father Abram, do you plan to stay at Shechem for just the rainy season, or . . . well, could this be the land God has promised you?"

"I don't know, Hagar. He hasn't told me yet. What do you think?"

Hagar again felt Sarai's eyes boring into her. She thought she knew what Sarai wanted her to say. She was tired of traveling. They needed a permanent home. And Abram would listen to Hagar.

But something within Hagar rebelled. Why do everything Sarai's way? Why not hers?

"I don't really know, Father Abram," she replied slowly. "For all I know, God wants you to go to Egypt."

"Egypt?" Again the sharpness in Sarai's voice. "Why Egypt? Just because that's where you were born?"

Abram's voice was gentle as he replied to her question. "It may well be Egypt. That might be why God sent you to us. I just don't know yet. I do know that God will speak to me and tell me what he wants me to know. If it's to be Egypt, he'll tell me. But in the meantime, we'll stay at Shechem for the rainy season. Maybe we'll know before the *malkosh* whether we should move on or not."

Sarai spoke, her voice still carrying a small sting. "Will you plant your crops there?"

"Probably. Unless God speaks to me otherwise, that is what I shall do."

Hagar frowned. This wasn't at all like Abram. Usually he made his decision in an intelligent manner, then ascribed it to God. This time his words implied his decision was separate and apart from what God said to do.

"Father Abram," she asked, "why do you

hesitate? Isn't God saying to you that Shechem is where you should stop for the rainy season?"

After more than a year in Abram's household, she had no fear that her bold question would be reprimanded. On the contrary, by now she felt secure in her position. In fact, she felt as though she were Abram and Sarai's only child.

Abram answered her gravely. "I really don't know, Hagar. I wish I knew when God speaks to me and when not. How much are my own thoughts and will, and how much are God's? It was more clear to me back in Haran than here in the land of Canaan."

"Is there some way you could ask God to speak to you?" Her question surprised her. She wasn't even sure why she asked it. Curiosity, perhaps. Abram's idea of a God speaking to him intrigued her.

"Maybe there is." Abram leaned back on the carpet, his hands behind his head, and gazing dreamily into the dark sky. "Maybe I could build an altar. Offer a sacrifice. Ask God directly."

Altar? Sacrifices? Hagar glanced at Abram, lying supine, his sharp nose and beard pointing upward. What was the man thinking of? He had never offered a sacrifice to his God before.

She knew a little bit about sacrifices offered to a god's followers, but that was usually jewelry or silver or food or fine clothing, which the priests then kept. Adherents of some religions offered animal sacrifices, trying to get their god to do something for them, or change their luck. She had even heard of human sacrifices made in the hope that a god would be impressed by such an important offering. But Abram had never mentioned sacrifices before. His God wasn't like any of those other deities.

Sarai spoke, her voice still clinging to the sharpness. "Why give God an offering? Does he need anything that you could give him?"

Abram chuckled and sat up. "No, of course not. That's not what I have in mind at all. I just want to show I have faith in him."

Hagar lifted her brows. "But doesn't he know that already? We know it. If it's clear to us, why wouldn't it be clear to God?"

Again Abram chuckled. "You're asking shrewd questions which I can't answer. I do know I need to show him that I believe in him, and thank him for what he has done for me. And maybe . . . just maybe he'll speak to me."

Hagar pursed her lips and looked away into the darkness. For the life of her, she couldn't despise Abram's faith. Sometimes it was silly and superstitious and rather naive, or at least it seemed so to her. But at other times, it made a lot of sense. Like now. A sacrifice for a noble reason, not trying to get God to do something. Just as an act of faith. Because Abram felt the need to do it.

Was this the thinking of a dreamer, a fanatic — or just a deeply religious person? If the latter, then she wished she could believe in a God like that.

10

Hagar stood with Sarai and the other women of the clan at the edge of the camp, watching the sacrifice. They were too far away to hear what Abram said, but in the still clear air they could see clearly.

Only the men were permitted to gather by the large oak tree, its gnarled trunk and branches seeming to preside over the proceedings. A few men remained with the flocks. But more than a hundred had gathered just east of the small town of Shechem, at the foot of an imposing mountain the local Canaanites called Gerizim.

Abram had repaired the ancient Canaanite altar near the oak tree, strengthening its sides so it now looked like a square mound. There he had built a large fire. When all was ready, he led the ram forward to be sacrificed.

The ram he held by the tether stood tall

beside him. To Hagar, it looked like two patriarchs, one human, one beast, staring at the large fire. The ram's horns curled around his head and pointed toward its shaggy back. Its face looked ancient and wise. The best ram of the flock.

Sarai had objected. "Why that one, Abram?" she had asked. "He has sired a large number of lambs in his lifetime, and he is still good for many years. And you are going to kill him? Why?"

"Because he *is* the best," said Abram cryptically. He would say no more.

Abram drew his knife for the sacrifice. From here on, he would do everything himself. Deftly he drew the sharp edge across the ram's throat. Blood spurted. Even from a distance, Hagar could hear the ram's startled bellow. It thrashed a moment before subsiding.

But that bleat, cut off by the gurgling of blood in its throat, sounded even at a distance like a cry of protest, as though the ram were asking the same question Sarai had asked him earlier: *Why me, my lord? You and I have been together a long time. We're old friends. Why are you slaying me?*

The blood poured on Abram's bare feet as he stood unmoving beside the dying beast. Perhaps he was talking to his bovine friend, explaining, apologizing, or comforting. Or praying? Hagar could hear nothing but the wind sighing in the trees. Everyone stood silent, waiting.

Finally Abram sighed, then stooped to cut up the carcass. Piece by piece, he heaved it onto the fire. He spoke words then, words Hagar could not hear. Was he speaking to God? Telling him this offering was from him, as a token of love and faith? Or was he saying to God, *I have spoken to you. Will you now speak to me?*

Suddenly Abram turned and walked away, in the direction of Mount Gerizim. Some of the men started to follow, but Abram waved them back. Soon he was lost in the trees which covered the mountain.

"Where is he going now?" muttered Sarai.

But Hagar thought she understood. He wanted to be alone, alone with his God. Perhaps he would select some high point on the mountain overlooking the valley which would give him a panoramic view of the scene. From high above, he could watch the smoke from the altar ascend to the heavens. In the stillness and peace of the height, he could listen for the voice of God.

When he did not immediately come back, the men under the large oak tree dispersed and went about their business. There were flocks to be tended. The women too returned to their daily work.

This was the middle of the rainy season. But there was no rain. The Canaanites who lived in this fertile valley between the two dominating mountains had been shaking their heads and muttering. They had not seen a season like this before. Normally rain fell in abundance. Grazing land was plentiful and crops grew with very little tending.

But not this year. Baal and Anat were helpless. Ordinarily the two gods would smile on the land of Canaan, sending rain, fertile soil, many crops, and prosperity. But not now. Maybe Abram's God had conquered them. Maybe they had run off to the north, to find refuge with the sky god at Mount Cassius. Maybe they had gone south to the city of Luz, seeking sanctuary in the house of El, leaving behind drought and famine and death. Or maybe they had died again this year. They had certainly forsaken the Shechemites.

Abram too had been concerned about the drought. The grazing areas, adequate for the scraggly flocks of the Shechemites in a normal rainy season, were now drying up. The shepherds had to move farther and farther away from camp seeking pasturage. The crops they had planted in the fertile valley had never sprouted. They had no more grain, and there was none to buy. The flocks were dwindling, producing less and less milk each day.

And God remained silent.

It seemed to Hagar that Abram was growing desperate in his need for divine guidance. The sacrifice, intended as an offering of love and thanksgiving, had turned into a plea for help. A last resort. A clutching at straws.

That was why Abram climbed the mountain. He would be listening for the voice of God.

He did not come down from the mountain that night. Hagar did not worry about him and slept well. But she could not fail to notice in the morning Sarai's red-rimmed eyes and drawn face.

"If he doesn't come down soon," she muttered, "we'd better send some men up after him."

He didn't come until late in the afternoon, just after Sarai had spoken to Mardi about sending out a search party. Sarai tried to look as though she had never been worried, greeting him formally and asking if he were hungry.

Abram's face was glowing. "I'm not hungry. I've had enough spiritual food to last me a long time." He laughed.

Hagar looked at him closely. He seemed radiant. What had happened up there? Had God spoken to him? Did he now know what God wanted him to do?

Abram would say nothing, however. He ate an early supper and went to bed as soon as darkness fell. Just before going to his bed, he called Mardi to him.

"We leave tomorrow," he said. "We're going south."

"South, my lord?"

"South, my friend. Looking for better pastures."

"But, my lord, our crops — ?"

"They'll never grow, Mardi. Not in this drought. And the grass is poor. Maybe further south, we'll do better."

Hagar frowned. Did that mean this was not the land God had promised him? Probably. That would be a land farther south. Egypt?

They left next morning, going down the ancient trail between the two mountains. The grass was sparse because of the drought, but Hagar could see that the land would be a good land, ordinarily green with pasturage at this time of year, arable and well-watered. It would be an excellent place to live when the rains fell on schedule. No wonder the local people called this a "land flowing with milk and honey."

As the days passed, Abram still said nothing. Yet he had an assurance in his step, a confidence in his voice, and a radiance on his face. He smiled and joked a lot. But he would say nothing of his plans.

A few weeks later, they arrived at Luz. There Abram built another altar and sacrificed one of his best he-goats. Afterward he told them what he planned to do.

They were encamped just east of Luz, a thriving city. Behind them the mountain ridge overlooked a valley, and a few miles to the west lay the ruins of an ancient city, called Ai by the Canaanites. The altar stood on a high point, and the men stood beneath another spreading oak tree. This time, however, Hagar and Sarai were close enough to hear Abram's words.

"Look around you," he said, his strong voice clear in the still afternoon air. "This is our home. All up and down these mountains we shall live. And our descendants shall live here for ever!"

Standing beside Hagar, Sarai gasped. "Finally!" she muttered. "We're going to settle down. Good. I'm ready!"

But Abram had not finished. Although he could not hear Sarai's soft words, his next words seemed to reply to her. "Tomorrow, we leave again. South. We shall eventually come to a country which has not been touched by this drought. Of this I have been assured by God himself, who spoke to me on Mount Gerizim!"

Hagar nodded. So God *had* spoken to him after all! How had he spoken? Did Abram hear a voice whispering softly in the mountain breeze? Had God heard the voice of Abram, raised so eloquently in the sacrifice of the ram on the altar at Shechem? Or . . . was this more of Abram's good sense in making decisions, which he so often referred to as God's will?

Whatever way God had spoken, the fact remained he *had* spoken. He had told Abram that this was to be the land promised by his God when Abram still lived in Haran.

Hagar looked around. This was beautiful country. She had been impressed by the rolling mountains ever since they had crossed the Jordan River. Although brown now, she knew it would be green and fertile. Springs dotted the area, flowing down into the valley. This place — and Shechem — would be an ideal place for Abram and his descendants to live.

But — Abram had said they would go south tomorrow. She glanced at Sarai, seeing her frown as she heard Abram's order for leaving the next day. Why move? If this were to be their new land, why pick up and leave it, now that they were here?

And then Hagar thought she understood Abram's reasoning. This was not the right year to settle here. They would need to go south, to a land not touched by drought. A land to support them this year, where sheep could graze and they could again plant crops. Then they would return. Then they would come back to this land Abram's God had given him.

She smiled at this thought. Abram's God. She no longer sneered at the idea of a God whom you couldn't see. This God, who was so real to Abram, just might be a living God, unlike the silly moon god and all those other idols. If so — if God did exist and spoke to Abram — maybe he would speak to her also!

But no, that was impossible. She was only a slave girl. A nobody. God spoke only to Abram. He never spoke to anybody else.

She gazed up at Abram, standing tall and proud, serenely watching the smoke from the sacrifice ascend to the sky. *He* believed. God spoke to *him*. For now, that would have to be enough.

11

Near the ancient city of Salem, they came upon a broad, fertile valley, well watered by a brook which flowed through it. Abram announced that here they would stay, at least until the *malkosh*. He spoke the word *malkosh* with a twinge of sarcasm, since the word literally meant "the last rain of the rainy season." There had been no rainy season this year.

Nevertheless, there would be adequate pasture here and also fertile land for the crops, except for one problem. There were Canaanites in Salem who claimed the valley was their own. They called it the "Valley of the King." The king to which it referred was the king of Salem.

This king sent word to Abram that he could not stay here. The valley, while rich in water, grass, and tillable soil, would not sustain so large an invasion and still provide a living for the people of Salem.

Abram sent back word that his people needed a place to stay for a few months. The sheep and goats were dying from too much traveling and too little water and grazing time. They had had no crop harvest for two years. And Abram made sure the king of Salem knew that staying was the will of Abram's God.

The day after Abram's message was delivered to the king of Salem, a small caravan of twelve asses loaded with sacks of grain appeared in Abram's camp.

The servant who seemed to be in charge of the caravan bowed low before Abram. He spoke in a highly accented but recognizable tongue.

"My lord the king," he said, "whose name is Melchizedek, offers you the hand of peace. As his name implies, he is a 'righteous king.' He will not allow anyone who visits our land to go hungry. Therefore he gives you this gift of grain, and he gives you permission to stay in this country for as long as you need to."

Hagar, from her position near the tents, could see the surprise on Abram's face as he opened one of the sacks. Wheat! Good, golden grains of wheat, from which much needed bread could be made. And enough seed crop for a future harvest! Surely Abram would believe this to be a gift from God and see this "Righteous King" as sent by God in their time of need.

Abram did not answer the servant immediately. Instead he walked around the twelve asses, staring thoughtfully at the generous gift. When he returned to the servant, he bowed courteously.

"Your king was properly named," he said slowly. "Will you give him an answer in the most respectful tone you can. I thank him with all my heart. His gift is most useful — no, more than that — vital. I cherish his friendship. And since this land, while rich, is small and will not sustain both his people and mine, I will move on. The God I worship will provide us, as he has already done through your king's generous gift."

The servant bowed, unloaded the grain sacks, and left with the twelve asses.

Abram gave his orders. "Save a portion of the wheat for seed. Make the rest into bread immediately. Use no leaven in the bread, for we will take it with us. We leave tomorrow. This is God's will."

That night the clan of Abram feasted on fresh bread. They had not realized until that moment how much they had missed this part of their diet.

Hagar disciplined herself to eat her allotment of bread slowly, so she could enjoy it longer. Though crumbly and heavy without the yeast, it tasted sweet, probably because they had done without it for so long.

In the flickering light from the glowing brazier, Hagar noticed that Abram and Sarai, who ate with her in the tent, were also savoring the unaccustomed treat. When a few crumbs fell on Abram's beard, Sarai, with a giggle, picked them off and ate them herself. "Mustn't waste it," she mumbled. Abram laughed.

This was the moment Hagar had been waiting for. She had something important to discuss with Abram and Sarai. "Father Abram," she began, speaking softly. "Have you decided on a wife for your nephew Lot?"

Abram frowned, "Has he been bothering you again, dear?"

"Oh no!" But she said it too quickly, and she sensed their disbelief. "Well, nothing I can't handle. He hasn't been rude. It's just. . . ."

Sarai shook her head. "That boy! He has grown up so fast! He certainly needs a wife."

"Yes." Abram finished his bread and licked his fingers. "And are you sure, Hagar, that you do not want him as your husband? It would be an excellent marriage for you."

Hagar knew what he meant. To be the wife of Lot, Abram's nephew, meant an end of slavery forever. More than that, it meant instant elevation to a position of honor, the matriarch of Lot's descendants. If Abram and Sarai died childless, it meant being matriarch of the entire clan.

"I know what it means, Father Abram. But I don't want to be Lot's wife."

Abram nodded. "I thought that was the case. Then it shall be as you say."

Hagar could not be sure, but she sensed that Sarai breathed a sigh of relief. She was again reminded of the mysterious purpose for her in the clan, which Sarai had hinted at but never explained.

Abram pursed his lips. "Now — what shall we do with Lot? Perhaps it is God's will that he be married to a princess, the daughter of a local king."

Hagar almost smiled at this. Her suggestion of several months ago, passed on to Abram through Sarai, had now become the will of God. But this was the way Abram reasoned; she was accustomed to it by now.

"Father Abram," said Hagar shyly, "do you know if this king of Salem has daughters? He seems such a good man."

Abram shook his head. "God has given him no daughters, Hagar. Only sons. But we'll keep looking. Someone's bound to turn up."

"Soon, I hope," said Sarai. "For Hagar's sake. Have you noticed, husband, how our little girl is growing up?"

Abram grinned. "I've noticed. She has become the second most beautiful woman in the world!"

The three of them, sated on fresh bread, relaxed and warm in their tent, laughed. Hagar felt a deep peace. In that moment, she felt closer to Abram and Sarai than she ever had to her real mother and father.

The next day, despite the grumbling among the servants and the listless movement of the livestock, they resumed their journey south.

Hagar noticed that Abram spent some time walking with Lot, and she guessed they were talking about marriage. Lot glared at her later and would not speak to her. And Abram sent Mardi out, after talking with him for a long time. Rumors circulated around the clan. Was he going wife-hunting for young Lot?

Later that evening, while Abram, Sarai, and Hagar ate their evening meal in their tent warmed by the coals in the brazier, Abram told them of his conversation with Lot.

"He wants to settle eventually in the Valley of Siddim." Abram munched thoughtfully on a piece of unleavened bread. "He has no liking for the mountains. That valley just south of the Salt Sea is where he would like to pitch his tent and pasture his flocks."

"Did you talk to him about marriage?" asked Sarai.

"Yes." Abram glanced at Hagar. "His first choice was you, my dear. He said he had developed a . . . small affection for you."

Hagar said nothing. Perhaps this explained why he was always looking at her, and finding moments to come and talk with her. She had never encouraged him, but he was persistent. That was only in the daytime, though. In the evenings, like tonight, he preferred to stay in his own tent with his herdsmen.

Sarai's question was one which Hagar would have liked to ask herself.

"And I suppose you told him Hagar wasn't interested in him?"

"Yes."

"And what was the young man's reaction to that?"

Abram frowned thoughtfully. "Anger, I think. No, disappointment. It was surely a blow to his pride to be turned down like that."

Sarai laughed shortly. "His pride! His lust, more likely. He's at an age when he needs a woman."

Abram nodded. "You're probably right. That would explain why he responded favorably when I proposed that we try to find a princess for him. He immediately suggested I try the kings of Sodom, Gomorrah, Admah, Zeboiim, and Zoar."

Hagar did not know where these cities — or kingdoms — were located, but she guessed they were in the Valley of Siddim south of the Salt Sea, since that was where Lot had said he wanted to settle.

Again Sarai spoke. "And I suppose that's where you sent Mardi? All kinds of rumors are floating around about that. Everybody guessed he was going wife-hunting, but they don't know where. Some said Beersheba, some said Gerar, and some even had him going all the way to Egypt."

Abram laughed. "Well, tomorrow you can tell them. The Valley of Siddim. Mardi is to go to each of them and negotiate. I gave him certain limits for his bargaining. Although I don't think the price will be too high.

"Any of those kings will be glad to make an alliance with us. After all, I can muster a hundred fighting men, well trained and well armed. They'd want my friendship. That's part of the bride-price, I suppose."

Hagar turned her head aside so Abram couldn't see her face in the flickering glow of the brazier. She frowned. All this talk about a bride-price, alliance, and negotiation sounded more like selling a goat than arrangements for marriage. She wondered if, when the time came for her to be married, she would be placed on the auction block and discounted and bargained for, like a woolly ram. Or like the slave market. Was that what daughters were for?

Then once again the thought occurred to her: what was her purpose in Abram and Sarai's scheme for her? Was it marriage? Was it an alliance? She would just have to be patient. Some day they would tell her.

12

They came out of the hill country south of Salem into a rugged plain which obviously — except for drought — would support large flocks and herds. The local people called it the *negeb*, although "dry land" was misleading. Abram, constantly studying the geography of the country by interviewing local inhabitants and caravans, had learned that the desert land came to life during the rainy season. Even in a time of drought there was enough rainfall to sustain a planting season of about two months. Beersheba, he had heard, had enough wells to sustain a large clan.

Beersheba was where Abram pitched his tents, hoping to stay a season or two while he waited out the drought.

The land was densely populated with migrating desert people and a fairly large city of Canaanites. Hagar was particularly interested in the name. "Beersheba" contained two Canaanite words, *well* and *seven*. The superstitious people said it meant "The Well of the Seven Demons." The more practical said it meant "The Seven Wells." There were more than seven now, but it might have been named many years ago when there were only seven.

But even Beersheba, with its many wells and lush vegetation, could not support the large influx of Abram's clan as they moved onto the best grazing land. Not now, when water was scarce. The local people were resentful, and only Abram's well-armed fighting men prevented open warfare.

"We can't stay here," Sarai told Abram. "But where else can we go?"

"Egypt." Abram turned to Hagar. "That may well be why God sent you to us, my dear. You shall lead us into Egypt."

"Me? But . . . Father Abram, I left Egypt when I was just a little child. How can I — ?"

"God will show us the way."

They could not leave yet, however. Abram had promised Mardi that he would wait for him at Beersheba. Meanwhile Mardi would tour the cities of the Siddim Valley searching for a suitable wife for Lot. And so they stayed through the Dry Season, waiting.

When Mardi finally returned, he brought good news.

"Bela, king of Zoar, has an eligible daughter. Her price is high. One tenth of all Lot's flocks must be given to him — now, and every year as long as they live there."

The price was too high, and Abram was inclined to refuse. Lot, however, felt differently. When he learned that Baara, daughter of King Bela of Zoar, was young and beautiful, he was eager to accept.

"In the Siddim Valley," he reasoned, "I'll be able to increase my flocks and herds tenfold. Then one-tenth of them will be the equivalent of what I own now, but I'll be nine times richer!"

"But Nephew, the bride price is not a one-time payment. It is each year for a lifetime, at least for as long as you live in Zoar. Can you increase enough each year to come out ahead?"

But Lot was eager to go. Everyone knew he did not like the rugged hill country of Canaan where Abram had decided to settle. Rumors of broad green valleys of abundant pasturage, fertile soil, and plenty of water attracted the youth. Hagar suspected the idea of cities and wealth and the prestige of marrying a princess was equally attractive.

At the time for the *yoreh,* Lot departed.

113

He took his sheep and goats and servants (inherited from Haran his father) and set out for a new life of prosperity and ease in the valley. Hagar was not sorry to see him go.

Nor were Abram and Sarai, it seemed.

"Now," said Abram, "there will be no more clashes between my men and his over whose sheep and goats belong to whom. This will surely make things easier for us when we travel to Egypt."

Sarai breathed a sigh of relief. "That boy! He could be exasperating sometimes! I never did feel he liked me."

Hagar would say nothing. But she too felt a lifting of the burden after he left.

The *yoreh*, the first rain of the season, never happened. Abram waited until several months into the rainy season before he made his final decision. The drought could not sustain them here, and the local inhabitants were growing more and more resentful.

"It is God's will," he said. "We must go to Egypt."

Abram chose to take the route through the Wilderness of Shur. Or, as he put it, God told him to go that way. If they followed the ancient caravan track, there would be sufficient springs and wells even for their flocks.

But they must move quickly from one oasis to another, because in between there was nothing but arid desert. Even so, it was the shortest distance to Egypt.

Although they left during the rainy season, there was no rain. Ordinarily a light rainfall fell in the Wilderness of Shur at this time of year. Not much, but enough for small pasturage.

Not this year. Abram pushed his flocks along as rapidly as possible, but they were weak and undernourished. Many died along the way. When they finally arrived in Egypt and crossed from the Red Lands to the Black Lands, Abram was not the wealthy man he had been upon leaving Haran.

God had spoken to Abram often through the caravan leaders he met on his way to Egypt, and Abram knew his geography. Zoan was the place God had told him to settle. The small city was on the eastern fringe of the broad delta of the Great River. It was surrounded by rich pasture lands. To the east of Zoan, the dust-gray desert looked lifeless. To the west, palm trees fringed moist fields of living green. The line separating the Red Lands from the Black Lands was obvious.

What fascinated Abram were the cattle, grazing in the well-watered pastures. He had seen them before, of course. They were well known in the eastern land he had come from. But he had never owned them. He told his family several times, "I must have some of those."

Hagar saw little of Egypt that she could remember from her childhood. Everything was such a vague blur to her. About all she did know was the language, and Abram summoned her often to translate.

One interview with a local person was particularly memorable. The man was a herdsman. His clothes were sparse. He had just one piece of dirty linen wrapped around his waist and hanging in careless folds to his knees. On his head he wore a head scarf, not as long as Abram's, and Hagar suspected he was bald underneath. His face was clean-shaven, as were most Egyptians, so unlike the bearded clan of Abram.

The man's name was Kh'Amun. He was old by Egyptian standards, perhaps fifty, his wizened face tanned and creased. He spoke volubly in a rural accent which Hagar found she could not only understand but speak fluently.

"What is your god?" asked Abram, his customary way of getting acquainted.

"I worship two gods, Great Sir. Amun, who is the greatest god of Egypt. And

Hapimu, the god of the Great River. They have been good to me."

Abram nodded. Hagar wondered if he would try to convert this Egyptian herdsman to his own religion, but Abram had other things in mind.

"Tell me about your cattle. Are they hardy beasts? What are they good for?"

There followed a lengthy discussion, tedious to translate, about the merits of cattle. Kh'Amun praised the strength of the oxen who could bear far heavier loads than the small donkeys which were Abram's beasts of burden. The quality of the meat was superior to both sheep and goats. And the milk! The simple herdsman actually became loquacious as he described the volume, the purity, the taste, and the healthy qualities of a cow's milk.

Abram next turned his attention to the people of Zoan. Were they friendly? Who governed them? Kh'Amun answered the questions patiently, telling about the wonders of that city, its marketplace, its merchants, its fine palaces with their gardens and fountains and hot baths. Hagar wondered how much he exaggerated.

"The pharaoh is there now," said Kh'Amun. "In the royal palace. But not Prince Senwosret. He is in Nubia."

"Does the royal family come often to Zoan?"

"Yes, Great Sir. Every year before the Flood. Especially in a year such as this, when Thebes is unbearable."

"In what way is Thebes unbearable?"

The old man scratched his nose. "The plagues. They happen every year, but are worse this year." He laughed. "They don't happen here."

"What are the plagues?"

Kh'Amun screwed up his face, thinking. "Mostly the red water. The Great River turns to blood. Fish die, frogs come out and die on the land, and flies come to eat the frogs. Wells go bad, and everything stinks. But it all goes away when the flood comes to the Great River again."

"Does the pharaoh always come to Zoan at this time?"

The man bobbed his head. "Yes, Great Sir. But you should be glad Prince Senwosret is in Nubia, guarding the borders." He grinned slyly. "When he's here, watch out!"

During most of the conversation, the herdsman had been facing Abram, ignoring Hagar as she translated. His last statement was addressed directly to Hagar.

Hagar translated. Abram asked the question she was hoping for.

"What do you mean, 'Watch out'?"

Kh'Amun sniggered. "That prince, he takes all the pretty girls in the country to his palace. Girls like you. Hee, hee! My own daughter, he took once. She came home pregnant! Hee, hee! Now my grandson is a son of the pharaoh!"

"But you say Prince Senwosret is not there now?"

"No. He's in upper Egypt, fighting the Nubians. But his father, Pharaoh Amenenhet, he does the same thing, only not as much as the prince. He takes only the prettiest. Hee, hee! Like you!"

Hagar shuddered as she translated. Abram became thoughtful as he listened and quickly brought the discussion to an end. Producing the usual gift of silver to be given to Kh'Amun, he thanked Kh'Amun for his friendship and willingness to provide them with information.

The herdsman volubly praised Abram with the most flattering compliments, most of which Hagar did not bother to translate. Then he hurried away clutching his silver coin.

Abram turned to Hagar. "You and Sarai must stay in your tent," he warned. "No coming out to greet visitors. Do you understand?"

"Yes, Father Abram."

She understood perfectly what Abram meant. He did not even need to issue the order for it to be obeyed. She hurried to Sarai to explain the problem.

Sarai was not as frightened as Hagar and Abram by this impending danger. She laughed. "What are they going to do, my dear? Send an army of men to fight against Abram, just to take us prisoner? Not likely! But I suppose we must stay close to our tent. What a pity! I was looking forward to shopping in Zoan."

Later, Hagar would be reminded of these prophetic words.

13

The people of Abram's household quickly adjusted to their new home. They had arrived shortly after the *malkosh* — though that term, they soon learned, didn't apply in Egypt, since there was little rainfall. The land seemed incredibly moist to Hagar, although she was told this was the driest season of the year.

The coming of the Flood was a new experience for the clan who were accustomed to constant dryness. The Great River swept out across the Delta, inundating the fields, bringing to the country life-giving moisture. The livestock, including the newly acquired cattle, scrambled to high ground and waited for the waters to subside.

When it did, the land blossomed. Green grass sprang up everywhere, and the animals gorged themselves. They began to fatten, to mate, to reproduce. Abram's wealth began to grow.

The people took advantage of the fertile, well-watered soil to plant their crops. The wheat crop, sowed from the carefully hoarded seed given to them by Melchizedek, produced abundant harvest. Soon bread was a daily routine. Onions and leeks spiced their meat, and they quickly learned to enjoy meals of beef as well as mutton and goat.

Fruits were plentiful, and the people were introduced to melons, oranges, and tamarinds, which became a daily part of their diet. Their vineyards produced grapes which were pressed into a rich wine. And from the Egyptians they learned to make a delicious beer from their grains.

Life was comfortable. Hagar could understand when God spoke to Abram and told him to stay here for two full years while he recovered his wealth.

Hagar herself grew into the full bloom of youth. Sarai often teased her about her beauty, although Hagar could not be sure if this was maternal love or jealousy. They kept to their tents, however; after Kh'Amun's warning, they never ventured to explore the marketplace at Zoan.

Abram continued to come to Hagar for advice. He still believed that somehow God spoke to him through Hagar. She gave him the best counsel she could. As her wisdom grew, she developed more and more confidence. And not just confidence — the seeds of power sown in her mind earlier were beginning to come to fruition. Not only was she flattered by Abram's turning to her for advice, but she became aware that he actually followed her suggestions more often than not.

Abram's wealth grew at an incredible rate during those two years. His new cattle herds extended across the pasture, and his men took the sheep and goats north and south seeking new pasturage. The local people began to resent them, perhaps jealous of Abram's phenomenal growth and prosperity.

Abram gave the credit to God. Hagar believed it was Abram's good sense and business shrewdness. The people of Egypt called it sorcery. They feared this powerful foreigner. Abram was forced to add more men to his already strong army. Soon he had over three hundred, skilled in the bow and arrow, the javelin and sword. Perhaps this, as much as the fear of sorcery, kept the local people at bay.

Abram was gone from their tents more and more, as he struggled to keep abreast of the business. His crops, his herds and flocks, and his men kept him out in the field for several nights at a time. Sarai and Hagar stayed at home, not daring to go anywhere. They tended the gardens, made linen clothing from the flax which grew abundantly here, and managed the growing number of household servants.

One morning Abram burst into the tent. He had been in the field for three nights, and they had not expected him back until tomorrow.

Immediately Hagar noticed his expression. Ordinarily he would be smiling and cheerful, but today his face was grave.

"What is it, Father Abram? What has happened?"

Abram tore off his headpiece. He still wore the long robes and headpiece of his ancestors, rejecting the more comfortable clothing of the Egyptians. "We must go home soon," he said.

Home? Hagar glanced at Sarai, but she shrugged and turned back to Abram. They both thought this was home, at least for a while. Of course, Abram had often stated his preference for the hill country of Canaan, but Hagar and Sarai had hoped God would lead him to stay here, where life was pleasant and prosperous.

"Why?" asked Sarai.

Abram sat on the carpet, and immediately Sarai served him a cup of wine. "A messenger has come from Lot," he said.

Lot! Hagar had forgotten about that boy — now a man — who had married and gone out of her life forever, she hoped. What now?

"Is he all right?" asked Sarai.

"For now." Abram sipped his wine slowly, obviously enjoying the rich flavor. "But there is war in the Valley of Siddim."

"Is Lot involved?"

Abram shook his head. "Not directly. But King Bela of Zoar, his father-in-law, is. Lot thinks he's in danger."

Hagar wrinkled her forehead. There were several small kings in that area. "Who's King Bela fighting against?" she asked.

Abram grunted. "They're all fighting, it seems. Five kings on one side and four on the other. Chedorlaomer, king of Elam, appears to be the strongest. And he's not on Lot's side. So it seems Lot thinks he is in danger."

"Does he want to come to Egypt?" asked Hagar, fearful of the answer.

"Yes. But I don't want to stay here. I shall send a message to him to meet us in Beersheba before the *yoreh*. We can move after our wheat harvest, and travel during the dry season, arriving in Beersheba before the first rain."

Hagar glanced at Sarai. She frowned. "Must we leave, Abram? We're so comfortable here."

"Yes," replied firmly. "God has given me the land of Canaan as our home. The hill country. Our descendants will live there forever."

At the word "descendants" Sarai stiffened. She glanced at Hagar, frowning. Hagar wondered what she was thinking. Sarai turned her face, perhaps not wanting Hagar to see the confusion in her eyes.

"I will stay here tonight," announced Abram, "and then tomorrow, I will make the rounds of the herds and flocks, alerting the men to our departure after the wheat harvest. This," he added mechanically, "is God's will."

Only a few months remained before the wheat harvest. There was much to be done. The gardens must be harvested, the donkeys assigned for duty, the household goods packed. Hagar could easily see the need for travel before the Flood of the Great River, when movement across country would be impossible.

The next morning Abram left early. The small town of tents became a flurry of activity. Orders were issued, and the familiar task of packing began again.

In the middle of their busy morning, a

small squad of Egyptian soldiers appeared outside their tent. When Hagar stepped outside to see what this new commotion was about, she was startled — and frightened. She estimated about twenty men, well armed, their long bows strung and ready.

"Mother Sarai," she called.

Sarai came out, and gasped. Her hand went to her mouth. She seemed about to scream. Hagar touched her shoulder lightly, and Sarai drew a deep breath and regained control of herself.

"What . . . what do you want?" she stammered.

The man who led them was obviously a noble, judging from his royal bearing. He bowed courteously.

"Greetings to the sister and daughter of the foreigner Abram," he said in a loud confident voice.

Hagar wondered briefly what the youth meant by referring to Sarai as Abram's "sister." But she dismissed the thought. Both in Haran and Egypt, wives were often referred to as sisters.

The officer continued. "I bring greetings from my father, ruler of all the Black Lands, Lord of Egypt, the mighty Amenemhet!"

Hagar caught her breath as she suddenly realized exactly who this youth was.

Senwosret, crown prince of Egypt. An energetic young man, he commanded armies in Nubia and defended the upper part of the Kingdom against invaders. Yet here he was in Lower Egypt, far away from where he was last reported to be.

The young prince was tall, smooth shaven, and dressed much like the herdsman Kh'Amun, except for his skirt and headscarf, which were made of the finest linen and shining clean. His smooth hairless chest was tanned by the sun. A handsome youth, he spoke with the air of someone who was not only accustomed to being obeyed but fawned over.

Hagar frowned. He probably was adored, especially by young girls. But not by her. She was cold to him as she spoke, translating Sarai's question Sarai had asked earlier. "What do you wish, mighty prince?"

"Why, your presence in the palace, of course. My father would be glad to receive you, and — "

He grinned, and the look of his eyes reminded her of Lot. "I too would be glad to welcome you."

"What does he want?" snapped Sarai, and Hagar translated. "Well, tell him we won't go with him. Who does he think we are, peasants?"

Hagar's words were as polite and respectful as she could make them, but there was no mistaking the abruptness in Sarai's voice. The youth looked at Hagar, then at Sarai, assessing the situation. He gave quick orders, and the soldiers surrounded the two women. They had no arrows in their bows, but they drew their swords.

"You must not refuse the pharaoh's invitation," the prince said sternly.

He gave more orders. The men grasped the arms of Sarai and Hagar and marched off with the struggling and protesting women toward the city of Zoan.

14

Only a few miles from Abram's tents they came to a large walled estate on the outskirts of Zoan. They entered through massive wooden gates into a dreamland.

A white palace dominated the estate. Only one story, it seemed higher than Abram's tallest tent. The house itself sprawled over an area in which all of Abram's tents could have been pitched. Against the sheer white of the walls, the four columns and balustrade which surrounded the door stood out in sharp blue, red, green, and beige.

They went through the open front door. They passed through a room with a high ceiling, again white with colorful borders. At the other end of the room they came outside onto a porch overlooking a garden.

The garden was dominated by a rectangular pool, mottled by green lily pads with white bulbs. Surrounding the pool were clumps of flowers and flowering shrubs. Behind them were several trees, some sycamore, some palm, and some bearing fruits of figs and dates.

Several children played in the garden. The boys, ranging in age from about four to ten, were naked, their heads shaved except for a pigtail sprouting on their right temple. The girls wore sheer linen dresses, and played with paddle-shaped dolls. Small dogs frisked among the children. Several cats preened themselves by the pool. Shrieks, laughter, and barks filled the garden.

A few women were there too. All but one were young and beautiful, wearing the same sheer dress as the girls. On their heads they wore the traditional black-and-gold wig of a wealthy Egyptian lady.

The older woman came toward them. She too wore white linen, though not sheer. She bowed low.

"Greetings," the prince said politely. "May Set smile on the good queen Sit-Hathor-Yunet this day."

"Thank you, my prince," replied the lady, whom Hagar would later learn was not the prince's mother, but another wife of the pharaoh who commanded the royal harem and nursery. "How may I serve you today?"

Prince Senwosret grinned and nodded toward Sarai and Hagar. "Two more. Take good care of them. Father and I will enjoy their company later."

His grin was more a leer than a smile. Again Hagar was reminded of Lot.

The prince and his soldiers departed, leaving Sarai and Hagar in the charge of Queen Sit-Hathor-Yunet.

The queen smiled, looking unexpectedly benevolent. "Please come with me, my dears. I shall try to make you as comfortable as possible."

She led them back into the palace and down a hallway until they came to a room Hagar could never have imagined. In the center of the tiled floor was a large pool. Three naked young women, aged about eighteen or twenty, stood waist deep in the middle. They were pouring water over each other using bowls.

The queen turned to her two charges. "Take off your clothes, please. You'll find this bath pleasant."

When Hagar translated this, Sarai frowned.

"I don't want to take off my clothes," she hissed. "It's not proper!"

"This is Egypt, Mother Sarai. Nudity is acceptable here, and common."

Hagar wondered how she knew this, then

realized she must have absorbed the knowledge in early childhood. She could recall being naked almost all the time as a child, which perhaps explained why she had not been too flustered by her nudity in the slave market.

After some persuasion, Sarai removed her clothes and they stepped into the water.

Hagar gasped. "It's warm!" She went down the steps into the pool until she came to the center where the three young girls stood. She smiled. "I like it!" Then she stooped down until the warm water covered her up to her chin, and Sarai followed.

Finally they emerged, and the young women helped them dry themselves on soft linen towels. But when the women brought out two white dresses for Sarai and Hagar, Sarai objected.

"I will *not* wear those scraps!" she said haughtily. "You can see right through them!"

Hagar spoke to Queen Sit-Hathor-Yunet, explaining Sarai's aversion to nudity arising from her cultural background. The queen seemed to understand. She graciously allowed Sarai to wear another dress. Although it revealed shoulders and arms, it was thick enough to cover the rest of her body. Hagar herself wore the soft sheer linen gown, which was both exotic and comfortable.

They were led to another room where they were seated on a bench in front of a mirror. Hagar and Sarai had seen their reflections in water, but never in a polished mirror. They stared for a long time at themselves. Hagar was both startled and gratified by her appearance. What she saw was a mature, strikingly beautiful, and poised young lady. She glanced at Sarai. Although several years older than Hagar, she too was stunning.

"Now, ladies," said the queen, "I know you look perfectly horrid to yourselves right now. What a shock that must be! But just wait. We shall make you beautiful."

The three women, who had followed them into the room, went to work on Sarai and Hagar. They brushed their hair and worked in perfumed oils until it glistened black in the mirror. Then the women placed wigs on top, so only a portion of Hagar and Sarai's real hair showed in the front.

Hagar winced. Her own shining ebony hair seemed far more attractive than the black and gold wig, which looked so artificial in contrast to the true hair.

Next the makeup. The first layer was a scented cream, followed by a black pencil which outlined the eyes and brows, and a red one which accented the lips. The smell of the perfume, at first sweet and attractive, became cloying and unpleasant.

Then came the jewelry. Necklaces. Girdles. And bracelets of gold and silver, cunningly inlaid with blue and green paste, carnelian, lapis lazuli, turquoise, amethyst, and garnet. To Hagar, the gaudy jewelry and makeup only detracted from the fresh beauty of the image she had first seen in the mirror.

"Beautiful!" exclaimed Queen Sit-Hathor-Yunet. "Don't you think so?"

"Yes, my lady," replied Hagar meekly, much too timid to tell the queen how she really felt about the artificiality of her adornment.

"Now," stated the queen in a satisfied tone, "you are ready to visit the royal bedrooms."

Hagar caught her breath. In the back of her mind, she had known the purpose of their abduction. But in the excitement and discovery of so many new things, she had forgotten.

"What will happen?" she asked, her voice quivering.

"I understand your nervousness." The queen's hand rested lightly on Hagar's shoulder. "You're a virgin, aren't you? I felt the same way my first time. But don't worry. I understand the prince is very gentle. And your mother has nothing to fear — the pharaoh is a master of love and pleasing a woman."

"But . . . but Abram — "

"He should be very proud. When his sister and daughter return to his tents, you will have inside your body the seed of pharaohs. Isn't that exciting?"

"What is she saying?" demanded Sarai, who could understand nothing of the conversation.

"She says you are Abram's sister, Mother Sarai. Should I tell her otherwise?"

"No."

Hagar raised her eyebrows. "But why not?"

Sarai frowned, creasing the makeup. Hagar made a mental note to remember not to frown.

"Abram and I talked about this earlier," Sarai replied. "We decided to pose as brother and sister. Abram spread the rumor among the Egyptians that we are not husband and wife."

"But . . . why?"

Sarai smiled, banishing the creases in the forehead but adding them to her cheeks. "Because they would probably kill him otherwise. Let's let them think that. Maybe Abram will be safe."

"But won't he bring his armed men to this palace and try to release us?"

"No, my dear. We agreed that if this happens, he would do nothing. 'God will take care of us,' he said. But I think the worst that can happen is that we'll submit to the pharaoh and the prince for a few weeks and then be released. That's better than Abram being killed and our staying here forever."

What Sarai said made sense. The key to Abram and Sarai's plan was survival. Hagar frowned. But she erased the frown after a glance in the mirror showed what it did to her makeup.

Another thought struck her. If they both went home pregnant, what then? Abram would have his son, his heir. Maybe that was also part of Abram and Sarai's plan. Abram would undoubtedly say it was God's will, that God had providentially arranged for this abduction and the impregnation of his wife. God's promise would be fulfilled, even if the child to be born was not the natural son of Abram. Hagar could imagine Abram's thoughtful comment: *God works in strange ways to accomplish his will.*

And Hagar would bear the child of a prince of Egypt!

Her mind went back three years, to the time when she had first come to the tent of Terah, Abram's father. She saw in her imagination the vivid picture of her kneeling at the patriarch's bed as he lay dying. He had blessed her. How many times had she gone over his words? She knew them by heart, and she could hear them now, echoing across the years.

You will live long, and may your womb be fruitful. You will be the mother of a great nation.

Was it possible? Would the prophecy of the dying patriarch be fulfilled in this way? She trembled with excitement. Strange things were happening to her.

Could this all be the will of Abram's God?

15

Only a few hours later, a servant brought word that Hagar — not Sarai — was wanted.

Sarai clasped her adopted daughter tightly, murmuring words of encouragement. Hagar, although fearful, did not dread this summons as much as she had thought. She kissed Sarai and left with the servant.

They went into the house and down a hallway, and Hagar again marveled at the ornate structure of the house. Even the hall was white marble. They entered through a large wooden door into a bedroom of sorts, only much bigger than Abram's largest tent. A huge canopied bed dominated the room, and a wide window opened onto the garden. Hagar glimpsed in the distance the reflection of the sun on the pool in the garden she had just left.

At one end of the room two people sat on

a double chair. The man wore a long linen robe which came up to his armpits, held around his neck by a golden pectoral with its sun disk representing Amun. His shiny black wig was plain.

The woman beside him wore a similar robe, cut low. Her wig was more elaborate, interlaced with precious jewels and topped by a golden tiara. She held a small fan.

Hagar looked closely at this couple. The man — could this be Pharaoh Amenemhet himself? And was she to be *his* bedmate tonight, rather than prince Senwosret's?

Before she left the garden, Queen Sit-Hathor-Yunet had instructed Sarai how to conduct herself in the presence of the pharaoh. Hagar followed the procedure now. She went to her knees before the man on the chair, and stretched out her hands at the level of his knees. "O king, live forever," she intoned.

The woman spoke. "Stand, child."

If this were indeed the pharaoh and his wife, then the woman was the renowned Queen Hathor-Hotpe, reputed to be the most beautiful woman in Egypt. As Hagar stood, she looked closely at the woman. Not even the heavy makeup could cover the age lines on her face.

Hagar then noticed two other men in the

room. The older man was obviously a scribe, sitting quietly, cross-legged, his papyrus and quills on his lap. The other, a young man, wore a plain skirt and short black wig. His features were sharp and hawkish, his eyes sunken.

The queen spoke curtly. "Physician!" The younger man stepped forward. "Examine her!"

The man stepped in front of Hagar. "Please come over to the bed," he said.

Hagar hesitated for only a moment. She knew she must obey. She lay on the bed, shutting her eyes and clenching her fists as the man did unspeakable things.

"She is truly a virgin," said the physician. "And clean."

As Hagar stood again before the pharaoh and his wife, she understood why the parents of Prince Senwosret would be interested in any foreign woman their son took to his bed. They were very protective.

The pharaoh's deep voice rumbled. "You are the slave of Abram and *habiru,* are you not?"

Hagar had heard the term *habiru* in Haran, used to designate an upper middle class of people who were military men, usually soldiers of fortune. She had never heard Abram called that before.

"Yes, sire." She spoke humbly, using the address she had learned from Queen Sit-Hathor-Yunet. "Only please, sire — he prefers the term *Hebrew*."

"Hebrew?"

"Yes, sire." She stared at the ruler's feet, careful not to look him in the eyes, which Egyptian custom forbade. "A descendent of Heber, son of Shem. Abram himself does not use the term, but others call him that."

"I see."

Somehow the great pharaoh of Egypt did not seem intimidating. Hagar glanced at his face. His keen eyes stared back. She saw in them no severity, only genuine interest.

"And what do you call your master?" he asked kindly.

"I call him 'Father,'" she replied softly.

"Father? But I thought you were his slave."

"I am, sire. Abram and Sarai have adopted me."

"I see. And his sister Sarai is your adopted mother?"

"Yes, sire." Hagar stared directly at the pharaoh. Something in the man's smiling face inspired confidence. Suddenly all fear of this exalted sovereign drained away. She spoke boldly. "Furthermore, sire, Abram and Sarai are not brother and sister. They are husband and wife!"

"What? But I have been told — "

"You were informed incorrectly, sire. They spread this story because they feared you would kill him and take Sarai for yourself."

"I see." The pharaoh frowned.

Hagar sensed she had gone too far. Now Abram would be killed. She wished she could take back all her words. But she could not. Once again she stared at his feet.

But he was not angry, as his surprising next question revealed."And what god does he follow?"

"Sire, my father's God has no name. In fact, he is the only true God. He is greater than all other gods, because he and he only lives."

Hagar wondered why she was speaking so boldly. A grunt from Queen Hathor-Hotpe drew her glance. She was frowning.

"Tell me, child," she said scornfully. "Is this God of your father's even greater than Amun?"

"Yes, madam."

"Even here in Egypt?"

"Yes, madam."

The queen's voice dripped venom. "And now you are going to tell us that the red tide which poisons the Great River was sent by your God without a name."

"Yes, madam."

"To punish us for separating Abram and Sarai."

"Yes, madam."

Why was she saying these things? She was putting Abram in great danger. Herself and Sarai too. She should take it all back. Now. Beg for forgiveness. Immediately.

"Sire . . . and madam — " She didn't know how to begin.

The Pharaoh interrupted. "This may well be true."

The queen turned to her husband and again spoke scornfully. "You can't believe that! This God is a foreign deity, and Amun is strong here in Egypt. Didn't he conquer all the other gods of Egypt? Doesn't he now rule all gods and command Hapimu, the god of the Great River, to come back to life? And doesn't he speak through you?"

But Pharaoh Amenemhet raised his hand, and she broke off her preaching. When the pharaoh spoke, others stopped talking and listened respectfully.

Now he spoke quietly, his composure reflecting inner peace. "Amun has spoken to me in a dream," he said. "At first I didn't know what foreign God Amun warned me about. Now I do. We must show him — and the man favored by this God — every respect. It *was* he who caused the red tide on the Great River, which killed Hapimu again this year.

"This nameless God will send on us great disease and famine and death unless we honor him. Let it be done."

The queen was silent. She only stared at her husband, and Hagar was aware of her respect (or awe, or fear?) as she nervously waved the fan she held in her hand.

Forgetting to stare at his feet, Hagar looked directly at the man in front of her. She had heard stories about him. He was the military commander of the Egyptian army who had overthrown the effete Pharaoh Mentuhotep many years ago. He had restored order and discipline to Egypt. Now he ruled his nation wisely and was respected not only in Egypt but by other countries as well.

He did not seem upset by the revelation that his own god Amun was inferior to a foreign God. Hagar wondered at the depth and strength of this man, who could lay aside his own religious convictions with such equanimity and accept the will of a foreign God. His convictions, yes — but also his ego, since the pharaoh considered himself a god. No wonder he was so revered by everyone.

But the awesome man in front of her was

not finished. "You and your mother shall be returned to the tents of Abram the Hebrew with your virginity intact. Permit us to send your father a gift, which shall arrive in a few days.

"Then, if it pleases his God, we bid him farewell. We will ask him to take his herds, his flocks, his servants, his wife and daughter — and especially his God — back to Canaan where he shall live out his days in peace." He turned to his scribe. "So let it be written, and so let it be done!"

Hagar gasped. In those simple words her entire life had been turned around. It wasn't just that their visit to Egypt was now at an end. There was more. Much more.

Abram's God had just spoken. It was as obvious as the next breath she took. The living God had just spoken. Spoken through the voice of the representative of Amun, the most powerful god of Egypt!

16

When Abram's clan arrived in Beersheba, Lot was waiting for them. As far as Hagar could tell, Lot had about the same number of sheep and goats as when he separated from Abram two years ago. Evidently the fertile pasture land of the valley of Siddim had not made him as wealthy as he had hoped. In fact, when Abram's vast herds and flocks invaded the broad oasis of Beersheba, now green and well watered since the drought had long since ended, Lot's wealth seemed puny compared to Abram's.

Hagar learned from Abram why Lot's flocks had not grown.

"That wedding bargain," declared Abram, "was not a one-time payment, but an annual assessment. Ten percent a year. No wonder Lot could not grow and get ahead."

"Doesn't the agreement hold?" asked Hagar. "Doesn't Lot still have to send yearly payments to King Bela?"

"Not any more," replied Abram. "That was one reason Lot wanted to move away and rejoin us. The original contract stated that the assessment would apply as long as he lived in Zoar. Moving was a smart move, although King Bela managed to confiscate half his livestock. Even so, he is now free to grow."

Lot had changed. A beard gave him a more mature look. He wore linen clothing, a cross between the scanty Egyptian garment and the flowing woolen robe Abram's people wore. Hagar wondered if this was the style of the people of Zoar, where Lot had chosen to live.

But something about Lot had not changed. When he came face to face with Hagar outside his tent, his eyes roved up and down her body, which now had filled out with adult curves.

"Well, well!" His voice contained the same sneer. "Our little *shifkhah* has grown up!"

Hagar bit back an angry retort. She was about to say that she was no longer a *shifkhah*, a favored slave, but *bas bayit*, an adopted daughter of the House of Abram. But why should she tell him that? Let him find out for himself.

"And how is your wife, Lot?" she asked,

ice dripping from her words.

Lot stared at her for a moment. She boldly returned his gaze. Lot was no longer smiling.

"What you need, *shifkhah*, is a good beating. I'm just the one to give it to you. And that's not all I'd like to give you."

The threat did not frighten Hagar. In the four years she had lived with Abram and Sarai, she had never seen them beat a servant. They would never permit Lot to do it.

But why should she stand here exchanging insults with Lot? She turned abruptly and walked away.

Later she met Lot's wife. Baara was pretty, with dark complexion, deep-set brown eyes, and jet black hair. And she was in her final month of pregnancy. Beside her was a two-year-old child. A girl. Lot still had no heirs.

Hagar also met Lot's concubine. She wondered why Lot, with both a wife and a concubine, still wanted Hagar. She would stay as far as possible from this family.

The two clans had not been reunited long before friction developed between them. Abram's wealth, especially the new cattle, seemed to arouse in Lot a deep jealousy. Abram offered him a bull and several cows to start his own herd, which Lot immediately accepted.

Following the *malkosh,* the last rain of the season, the lambing season began. Confusion arose as to which lambs and kids belonged to whom. Abram graciously conceded most of the disputed offspring to Lot, but it seemed to Hagar his nephew took advantage of his uncle's generosity.

"It's time to move," announced Abram one day. "We have outgrown Beersheba."

The patriarch had always preferred the high country, feeling the land promised him by God lay in the mountains between the *negeb* and Shechem. Now that the drought was over, there were many good areas of upland pasture, and Abram was eager to move on. He planned to spread his flocks and herds across many miles of upland.

Lot resisted. He hated the mountains. His first choice was the valley of Siddim. There, he claimed, grass grew faster than the livestock could eat it. Several times he spoke of returning to the cities of the plain. This despite the threats from Chedorlaomer, king of Elam, whose announced purpose was to conquer the entire Siddim Valley.

As the friction between the two clans grew, Abram made a generous offer. He sent a message to Chedorlaomer that his nephew Lot was under his protection. If any threat from Elam endangered Lot, Chedorlaomer would have to answer to the wrath of Abram.

This was no idle threat. Abram now had a small army of more than three hundred fighting men. Abram had developed this unit himself. They had been trained in the use of bow and arrow, sword, and spear by Mardi, who had learned the martial arts as a youth in the service of the Babylonians. Chedorlaomer would think twice before challenging Abram.

With this assurance, Lot made the decision once again to part company with his uncle. This time, however, he would not return to Zoar, where his father-in-law Bela ruled. He did not want to resume his annual assessment. Instead, he declared, he would live in Sodom, one of the richest cities of the Siddim Valley.

Hagar breathed a sigh of relief at Lot's decision. His clan was now considerably more wealthy because of Abram's generosity. Before they left, Lot's wife Baara delivered her second child. A girl, much to Lot's disgust.

"We'll try again," he announced. "Sooner or later, I will have an heir."

Lot's announcement was a slap in Abram's face. Sarai seemed hopelessly barren, unable even to produce a girl. Hagar noticed how Abram squared his shoulders and compressed his lips at Lot's thoughtless pronouncement.

Then they were gone, and Abram's clan once again resumed their nomadic ways. They moved northward, into the hill country Abram loved so much.

Hagar found it enchanting also. The drought was gone, and the *yoreh* brought the first rain of the season, turning the land into a green paradise. Oaks and pines and terebinths covered the rugged hills. The goats feasted on the acorns while the sheep and cattle cropped the abundant grass. Streams flowed down the hillsides, and everywhere a variety of flowers splashed colors among the greenery.

Abram distributed his flocks and herds along the ridge between the *negeb* on the south and Shechem on the north. Everywhere he planted gardens, expecting a large crop of wheat after the *malkosh*.

The years passed blissfully. Abram moved his tents from Bethel to Shechem to Salem to Beersheba, enjoying the land. His wealth grew, until he became the richest and most powerful ruler in the region. Unlike the other wealthy men who lived in the land of Canaan, Abram never referred to himself as a king. To him, only God was the sovereign ruler.

Abram restored several Canaanite altars and offered many sacrifices. He declared again and again that God had given him this land. His descendants would live here forever. That he believed this was obvious, but Hagar had her doubts. Sarai was barren. Did that mean that the descendants of Abram would be the children of his servants? Would Mardi — Mardi's son Eliazer — become the patriarch of the clan at Abram's death?

Or . . . Lot? Hagar shuddered. If that happened, then Hagar might revert to being a slave, a concubine for the lusts of Abram's nephew. But Lot had no sons, only two daughters. Would he perhaps marry Hagar, thus making her the mother of the descendants of God's Promise?

If so, she would fulfill the deathbed prediction of Terah, Abram's father, who had promised that her womb would be fruitful and she would be the mother of a great nation. Would that be the way Abram's God would keep his promises? She shook her head. She still didn't want to marry Lot.

Then Lot entered their lives again.

King Chedorlaomer of Elam had moved out against the cities of the Siddim Valley. With some he made an alliance; with others, including Sodom and Zoar, he fought.

Foolishly he ignored Abram's warning to leave the family of Lot alone. Instead he absorbed Abram's unfortunate nephew and his wealth in his sweeping conquest.

Abram kept his promise. He aligned himself with the kings of Salem, Shechem, and Bethel, and set out to rescue Lot. Sarai and Hagar worried during his absence, but he soon returned, bringing with him Lot and his family after completely vanquishing King Chedorlaomer.

But Lot refused to live in the hill country. Once again he moved back to Sodom, where he could now live in peace because of Abram's conquest of the king of Elam.

And the blissful years continued.

Hagar had matured into full womanhood. The few times she had raised the issue of marriage with her adopted mother, she had been put off. "Not yet," was all Sarai would say.

Sarai herself was aging. The fabled beauty which had attracted attention everywhere, even in the courts of Egypt, was fading. Little lines appeared on her face and neck, and her hair turned gray. Her body began to dry up, and she could no longer bear children. What of God's Promise to Abram concerning his descendants?

One day Sarai and Abram argued. This

shocked Hagar. Her adopted parents never argued. Although they did not raise their voices, they were clearly in disagreement. When Hagar approached, they fell silent.

But they were not silent long. Sarai spoke, her voice snappish.

"I say the time has come, Abram. Now."

"No."

"Yes. Now. It must be."

"No. God will keep his promises."

Hagar stood beside them, feeling as though she had come into the argument in the middle, or more likely at the end. Both of them had made up their minds. There seemed no room for further discussion. They were just restating their positions.

But what were they arguing about?

Ten years ago she would have retired shyly and waited until her master and mistress had settled their dispute. Now she stood firm, waiting until her parents brought their daughter into the discussion.

Abram and Sarai glared at each other. Hagar looked in dismay from one to the other. The conviction grew within her that she must take part in whatever their disagreement was because she was part of the family.

"Please tell me," begged Hagar. "What are you talking about?"

Both Abram and Sarai turned to stare at Hagar.

"Shall we tell her, husband?" asked Sarai.

"No."

"Yes."

"Then let's ask her to settle it for us."

"No. This is my decision." Sarai's lips tightened, and muscles moved in her face.

"It is God's decision." Abram's voice matched Sarai's severity. "It is he who has promised — "

"And this may be his way of keeping his promises."

Hagar sighed. "Please!" she broke in. "Tell me what this is about. Maybe I can help."

"Yes," said Sarai.

"No," said Abram.

"I'll tell you anyway." Sarai glared at her husband. "Don't try to stop me, or I'll just tell her at another time."

"But Sarai — "

"*What?*"

Abram bit his lip. His eyes went from Sarai to Hagar, and back to Sarai. "Well, in that case, I'm leaving. You can tell her without my being here."

"Maybe that's just as well." Sarai nodded. "Yes. I'll talk to you about this later."

Abram turned and stomped off.

Hagar's curiosity was by now ready to explode. She turned eagerly toward Sarai. But her adopted mother was in no hurry to talk.

"Come with me, Hagar," she said. She turned and strode away from the tent.

Hagar caught up with her, and together they walked into the forest. Sarai led her to a towering oak tree, a favorite spot for both of them, since it offered them shade, a view of surrounding hillsides, flowers, and peace. Sarai seated herself on one of the massive roots, and Hagar sank to the mossy ground before her.

For a long moment Sarai regarded her daughter. Hagar waited patiently, knowing that soon she would learn what had so divided Abram and Sarai.

Sarai sighed. "I don't know how to begin. Do you recall when I first purchased you in the slave market in Haran?"

"Yes, Mother Sarai."

"I bought you for a specific purpose."

Hagar had forgotten. In the early years she had been aware of a specific purpose for her life, but as time slid by she had settled so comfortably into the role of daughter that she had forgotten all about that. Now it came back to her. What was her purpose?

"I'm growing old," continued Sarai. "I don't think I can have children any more."

"Oh, Mother Sarai. . . ." Hagar didn't

want to say. She could guess what anguish these words brought to Sarai. That she could give Abram no sons had been the only dark shadow in her life. And it meant so much to her.

"But in a way, I can have children. Hagar, you shall bear my children for me!"

"Me? But how — "

"You know very well how. Haven't you known this for the past ten years?"

"No. . . ."

"It's time you know now. I want you to go to Abram's bed. Let him sire a child through your body. That's why I bought you in the first place."

Hagar gasped. "No! No, Mother Sarai, I couldn't! I — Abram . . . why, he's my father! I couldn't!"

"He's not your father. He's your master. You are his slave. His *shifkhah*. That was your purpose from the beginning."

"Oh!"

Tears welled in Hagar's eyes. She should have guessed. Why hadn't she? Because Abram was too much of a father to her? She could never think of him as her lover.

Lover! The thought was repulsive. Abram. Her father. Her lover. Tears streamed down her cheeks.

"Oh, Mother Sarai, I couldn't!"

"You can. You will!" Sarai's voice was sharp. "Furthermore, the child will be mine."

"Oh!"

Suddenly it became clear to her. The custom had been established long ago among the people of the East — children born to a handmaid, a concubine, a *shifkhah*, would legally be the children of the wife. Hagar would be the natural but not the actual mother. Her body would be used. The child would pass through her but never belong to her.

It was too much. She bent her head, put her hands to her face, and sobbed. "No. No. Please, Mother Sarai, don't make me do this — "

Sarai's voice softened. Her hand rested gently on Hagar's head. "Dear child," she murmured. "It has to be. This is God's will. How else can he fulfill his promise?"

How indeed. She could not fight against the will of Abram's God. But this God — this benevolent deity who shaped and guided the lives of his people — why would he do this? Why not just use his powers and make Sarai fertile? Why destroy the life of her daughter? No, not her daughter. Not any more. Her *shifkhah*. Her slave. Her handmaid, whom she could order to Abram's bed.

Hagar shuddered. Was this how Terah's dying words would be fulfilled? Would *she* be the mother of Abram's descendants?

But she couldn't be. Even if she bore a son, it wouldn't be hers. It would be Sarai's.

God! she shrieked inside her mind. *If you are a God. Don't do this to me! Please!*

17

For several years, Hagar had lived in a tent of her own, separate from Abram and Sarai's. She knew it was an indication of her favored status, not as a *shifkhah*, but as a daughter.

Hagar prepared herself for her first night with her father Abram. She shuddered. Not her father. Her lover. Her master. The man who would rob her of her virginity, her place as daughter of the House of Abram, and eventually of her child.

She had discussed this earlier that day with Abram. He was as reluctant as she to share her bed. But Sarai had the right to offer her *shifkhah* for this purpose. While Abram also had the right to refuse her, he would not.

"It's important," he had explained to Hagar, "for both of us. Surely you can see that."

Hagar did understand. Sarai, childless, was a failure as a wife. Abram, childless, would be unable to fulfill God's promise. For both of them, surrogate motherhood through their *shifkhah* was the only logical solution. It would be good for everyone — except Hagar.

She wondered how she would ever fulfill Terah's deathbed prediction. He had said two things. Her womb would be fruitful. That might well come true. But that she would be the mother of a nation . . . that was now impossible. She would be the mother of Sarai's nation.

Hagar sighed. Just a few days ago, she thought of herself as a *bas bayit,* daughter of the House of Abram. She had looked forward to being an *asha,* wife of some important person, honoring that man with children who would become a mighty nation. Now she was reduced again to *shifkhah,* handmaid to her master.

But her tears were over now. Hagar had resolutely determined to bear her suddenly lowered status with dignity. It was much like those months just after she had become a slave. She had faced a decision then — either die of sorrow or accept her situation and live it to the fullest. She had chosen to live. She would also choose now to live.

In spite of this decision, she was smoldering with anger against Sarai. Not against Abram. It was Sarai who was spoiling her life. Abram was not to blame. She must rid her mind of any resentment against the man who had become a father to her. And do all she could to make this experience easier for him.

But first, she must banish from her mind the idea that Abram was her father. He was not. No more. He was her lover.

She had carefully bathed herself today, cleaned her tent, prepared her couch with fresh linen, and put on her best clothing. She refused to think of the ordeal Abram would put her through as she lost her virginity.

"Hagar."

He was here. Abram lifted the flap of her tent and stepped inside.

Like Hagar, Abram had prepared for this night. He had bathed, dressed in a new robe, and oiled and brushed his hair and beard until they shone. Hagar felt flattered by this.

He seemed as nervous and unsure of himself as she. They stood there in the tent, staring at each other. The oil lamps dimly lit the interior, obscuring the bright colors she had chosen to bring joy and pleasure to her home.

Abram remembered to remove his sandals just before stepping onto the carpet. He seemed almost apologetic.

An awkward silence hung between them. Hagar was aware that, in spite of Abram's maturity and experience as a lover, he was as embarrassed and shy and hesitant as she was. She felt vaguely guilty, as though she were committing incest. Did Abram feel the same?

She smiled. "Abram," she murmured.

That she had dropped the usual "Father Abram" was instantly obvious to him, for he nodded.

"Hagar, my dear," he replied, avoiding the phrases "my child," or "my daughter," which he had so often used in the past.

She decided on boldness. If he was as guilty and uncomfortable as she, he would be grateful for any help she could give him.

"Welcome to my tent," she said, smiling. "And to my bed."

Her shameless, almost brazen statement had its effect on the man standing before her. He smiled, his face relaxing. Some of the tenseness went out of his shoulders. Perhaps he was jolted into a reminder that his role as the man was to take the lead in their lovemaking, to assert himself as the experienced lover, to put her at ease rather than the other way around.

He stepped closer and reached out for her. She came into his arms, which went around her in a soft embrace.

She lifted her face to his, and his lips found hers. She had never experienced this before. Always in the past, he had kissed her cheek. Now, it was his lips on hers. She did her best to respond. This was her lover. Not her father. Her lover. Her lover.

When it was over, Abram kissed her tenderly. "Thank you, my dear," he said softly. Then he rose and put on his robe. "I'll be back again tomorrow night."

He left then, leaving behind a bewildered young woman. She had expected him to stay for the entire night, to make love to her over and over again. Instead, he had gone. Why? Had she failed him somehow?

The tears came then. She huddled on her bed, sobbing. Something deep inside her brimmed over. She whimpered, trying to stifle the wail that rose in her throat.

After a few moments, her turmoil subsided. She forced her mind to recall some of the tender moments they had experienced, and that soothed her. Still she was confused.

She recalled a ram she had watched just recently copulating with a ewe. A familiar sight. The same with goats and cattle. One intense moment of frenzy, almost unfeeling, without love and tenderness. So different from a coupling of two humans. Abram had filled those few moments with gentleness and affection. And sensitivity. He had been very much aware of his concern for her feelings. He had been patient and, though aroused, never brutal.

Perhaps it was understandable that Abram had left her tent. He was old. One round of lovemaking would be enough for tonight. Tomorrow she could look forward to the same. One time. It could not be too difficult. It was common knowledge that the pain of destroyed virginity lasted only for the first time. After that, some people said, it even became pleasant.

And he had gone back to his own tent. Sarai's tent. Why not? That was where he belonged. Sarai would be there, waiting for him. How would she feel? Jealous? Unhappy? Would she want him to make love to her now, just to prove that he truly loved her, and not the *shifkhah* with whom he had just done his duty?

His duty! What a way to think of this experience, so surrounded by love and affection! Duty was what a ram would do. But surely this act of love was not just a duty!

Impossible. This was a fulfillment of love

between a man and a woman, resulting in the birth of a child. That was the way a wise and benevolent God had created them.

After ten years of living in Abram's tents and hearing him talk about the God who spoke to him, she had come almost to believe in this God. If only he would speak to *her!* He was everything she wanted a God to be — loving, wise, trustworthy.

He was the kind of a God who would create a man and woman for love. When a man and a woman came together to sire a child, it was more than just a satisfying of carnal appetites. It was love. A soft, delicate moment in which they shared affection, understanding, and consideration. How thoughtful Abram's God had been to give to his people this marvelous way of having children.

But suddenly she frowned, as an unpleasant thought crept into her mind. It was not her child Abram would sire through her with such love and gentleness. It was Sarai's.

It wasn't fair! This was not what God had intended for his creatures! If a child was born of this union of love, it should be hers, not someone else's! Otherwise the act of love created by God for having children would be meaningless. She might as well be a ewe serving a rutting ram.

But she wasn't! She was human, and if their love produced a baby, that child should be hers!

She sat up in her bed. Was that possible? Could the child which came from this union of love be hers after all? Could she somehow work that around to becoming the will of God?

Why not? Wasn't that what Abram always did? He thought through a situation carefully, planned well, made intelligent decisions, then claimed it was God's will. Why couldn't she do the same with any seed Abram had planted inside her? Yes. It would be God's will that the child be hers.

But how? The answer was instantly obvious. After all, she had lived in Abram's tents for ten years. She well knew how her father — master — lover — thought about God's will. God often spoke to him through Hagar. Several times she had planted in Abram's mind an idea, and it had grown there until it bore fruit. According to Abram, it was God's will.

Could she plant in his mind the seed that God wanted Hagar to be his wife? That any children born to her would be her own, not Sarai's?

But how? By subtle suggestions. By sly questions. *Is it possible that God intended all along that I should be your wife? Maybe God meant for this child to be mine, not Sarai's.*

Would Abram accept that? He was not stupid. He had only one blind spot, his need to see all his intelligent decisions as God's will. If she could play on this blind spot. . . .

But she would have to be careful. The suggestions must be subtle. Barely a hint. Drop a small thought into his mind and let it grow. She had done it before. She could do it again if she was careful.

Toward Sarai, she would be humble and submissive. *Your child is growing within me, Mother Sarai. I hope you will teach this child that I am his beloved Aunt Hagar.* Yes. That was how she would handle Sarai.

And her subtle hints to Abram? Dropped into his mind only when Sarai was not around. Perhaps in his arms, while he was making love to her. That, she had heard, was when a man was most vulnerable.

Hagar smiled, nodding her head. She could fool Sarai. She could fool Abram. And God? Was she deceiving God?

If so, perhaps he would speak to her. And if she had her way, God would tell her the child of this union of love would be hers!

18

Hagar had been right. The first time was the only painful experience. After that, it grew more pleasant.

She didn't know which she liked better — the gentleness of Abram or the pleasurable sensations. Somehow they blended, and each night provided new excitement. She began to experiment with new ways to make their lovemaking more pleasing to Abram, discovering that this also made it more pleasant for her. Love, she decided, was a shared experience.

How wise was Abram's God, to enhance and surround the process of continuing the race with such an enriching and satisfying relationship! She wanted it to go on and on, for the rest of their lives together.

Each night, as she lay with her lover, she whispered into his ears endearing words. Words filled with subtle hints. Words carefully chosen during the day and calculated to fix an idea in his mind.

"Abram, my love, isn't it wonderful that we can lie here together as husband and wife?"

"My dear, how lovely this experience is! Your God is kind and thoughtful, to enable me to be mother of your son."

"I wonder, my love, just what God plans for me. Remember when Terah predicted that I would be the mother of a nation?"

Abram seemed not to reject the hints. Indeed, all his responses were tender expressions of lovemaking. Perhaps the seed she had planted in his mind was bearing fruit. Perhaps not. She didn't know. She needed more time.

But it could not last, she well knew. Through the long days, while she waited the coming of her lover to her tent, she thought about that.

When she became pregnant, the visits would cease. And if she produced a son, she would never share her bed with Abram again.

She approached her monthly "time of the women," as Sarai's people so delicately phrased it, with dread. Was she pregnant? Had Abram's seed already formed in her body to build for him his son and heir? She

171

prayed it had not. *Abram's God, please! Give me more time!*

Abram's God, if he really existed, did not answer her prayer. She was pregnant. She had never deceived her master and mistress, but now she would.

"Abram," she whispered to him, as he was about to leave her tent one night, "don't come tomorrow night. Nor for two days after."

Abram looked at her, his eyes under lowered brows sad. Finally he sighed. "I had hoped. . . ." He shook his head. "All right. I will return on the fourth night."

The next three nights were long and lonely. Even though Abram only stayed in her tent for a brief time, their moments were deeply fulfilling to her. Now the three nights of his absence were filled with depression and tears. Only thoughts of the renewal of bliss on the fourth night sustained her.

She felt sure she had deceived Abram, but she didn't know about Sarai. Often she caught Sarai's frowning glance. She avoided her mistress as much as possible.

Finally the period of deception and waiting was over, and she was joined to her lover again. It seemed to Hagar that her joy increased. Each nightly experience, although brief, left her glowing and warm on her couch.

But it could not last.

When the second month had passed, and her "time of the women" drew near, she again prepared to deceive her lover. She might have succeeded had it been only Abram. But Sarai would not be fooled.

One morning, just outside her tent, she found Sarai waiting for her.

"Abram won't be coming to your tent any more," she snapped.

"Why not?"

Sarai sniffed. "Don't give me those innocent eyes, you liar. You know why not. I hope it's a boy. Then he'll be through with you forever."

She turned and walked away, stiff-legged.

Hagar sighed. So it had come to an end. So soon. But she had had two months. Two wonderful months. Two full months of love.

Now, if only the child growing inside were a girl. . . .

Hagar was not prepared for the misery that invaded her life during the next few months.

Loneliness assailed her. She missed the nightly visits of Abram, although she could not understand why. Was it because she had become addicted to the joys of sex? Or was it something else — some feeling for Abram she didn't fully understand?

When she saw Abram during the days, he seemed embarrassed even to talk with her. Did he feel the same toward her as she toward him? Was it merely loyalty to his wife that kept him from seeking her out?

Or . . . was it possible that their tender coupling meant nothing to him? Was he just "doing his duty"? But that was impossible. They had said things to each other . . . found secret ways of giving pleasure. . . .

No. It must be Sarai. She had probably poisoned his mind against Hagar. It wouldn't be difficult. Sarai would constantly remind him that she was his wife, and Hagar was the *shifkhah* through whose body their child would come. *Our son,* she would say. *Your heir. The way God will fulfill his promise.*

But what about all those hints Hagar had dropped into his mind during their nights of lovemaking? Had they borne fruit? Or had Sarai's poison killed them?

Hagar's loneliness was not only for Abram, but for Sarai also. Sarai had changed. No longer was she the companionable mother with whom Hagar shared laughter and long moments of serious conversation. They still worked together in the camp, but their relationship was cold.

With no one to talk to, Hagar turned inward. She brooded. She tried to talk to Abram's God, but as always he seemed to shut her out. Maybe he talked to Abram — and maybe he didn't. She didn't know. One thing she did know. He didn't speak to her.

The baby was growing inside her. She could feel the changes in her body. She watched in awe as her stomach began to swell, and she became aware of slight movements. The child was alive! Was it a boy? The fulfillment of Terah's prediction? Or was it a girl?

She hoped it was a girl. Then Abram would come back to her tent. Then she could feel the warmth of his love, his gentle caresses, his whispered words which meant so much. Then too, she could continue her campaign to sow in his mind the seeds of doubt. Perhaps she could yet convince Abram that God meant for Hagar, not Sarai, to be the mother of the great nation. That was what Terah had predicted. Perhaps that was what God's Promise had meant.

But she was daydreaming again. Having a baby inside of her made her feel soft and dreamy. She had almost forgotten the horrible reality. If it was a boy, he would be taken from her. And she would be nothing. Not a mother. Not a lover. Not a daughter. Nobody. Just another slave.

She must not let that happen!

What could she do? Where could she turn?

To Abram. Yes. She would find a way to talk to him. When Sarai was not there. What would she say? *Your son is my son, Abram. I am your wife just as much as Sarai. That is God's will.*

Would he listen? Or had Sarai so poisoned his mind and prejudiced him against her that no words of hers would make a difference? If so, she had nothing to lose by trying.

The chance to speak privately with Abram did not come until the seventh month of her pregnancy. The clan was encamped at Beersheba, since Abram had some business with Abimelech, king of Gerar. They had met in the large oasis in the *negeb*. Sarai was gone, calling on the family of the visiting king.

Hagar selected her moment. Abram and Abimelech had finished their business, and the king had just left. It would be some time before Sarai rejoined them in Abram's tents.

"Abram?"

She stood outside his tent, calling to him. A moment later, he lifted the tent flap.

"Yes, Hagar?"

He had removed his head covering and his outer robe. His hair and beard were not freshly combed and oiled. Perhaps he was preparing to relax in his tent and rest. She wondered if she had chosen the best time.

"May I talk with you? Please?"

He hesitated, but only for a moment. "Of course, my child. Come in."

She noted the use of the phrase, "my child," wondering if he was deliberately reverting to their father-daughter friendship to avoid the relationship of lover to lover.

She removed her sandals and came in. Abram sat on the carpet, motioning her to do so as well. Clasping her hands tightly in front of her, she sat primly on a pillow and gazed at the carpet before her.

"Now, my child, what is it you want to talk about?"

His voice was smooth, showing no signs of embarrassment. A glance at his face told Hagar he was nothing more than a loving father eager to help his daughter with whatever problem she laid before him.

"Abram, if this child. . . ." She patted her swollen belly. "If this is a boy, and . . . and he is your heir — "

Abram smiled. "I'm sure he's a boy, Hagar. God keeps his promises."

"Yes. A boy. Your heir. Abram, what shall become of me? Do you have plans for my future?"

"Hagar, don't worry." His voice held the same tenderness she so vividly remembered from their nights of lovemaking. He was different when Sarai was present. "We haven't forgotten you. After the child is weaned, I'll find a suitable husband for you."

"Oh, please, Abram. I don't want another husband. I want . . . I want — "

"Come on, child. Say it. What do you want?"

Hagar took a deep breath. "I want to be *your* wife!"

As soon as she said it, she lowered her eyes to the carpet. He was silent. Had she moved too fast? Yes. There must be something more which she must say. And she knew what it had to be. She said it without lifting her eyes.

"I think, I believe — that's what God wills for our lives!"

There. It was said. Now he could either reject it forever, or give her a new life. But it was said. She had laid it before him. The choice was his.

She knew exactly what she asked of him. To be his wife. Not his *shifkhah*, the surrogate mother of his son. His wife. His *asha*. The equal of Sarai. If he granted that, then the son born to him would be hers, not Sarai's. And she, not Sarai, would be the mother of the children of the Promise.

"You're asking a great deal, my child. Why?"

His voice was gentle and encouraging. She raised her eyes from the carpet and looked at him directly.

"Because I — because I don't want to live in someone else's tent. I don't want to make love to anyone else. I want to make love only to you. And I think this is God's will."

He frowned, but she had no idea what went on behind the bushy brows. She dropped her eyes to the carpet again, assuming the pose of a humble woman.

The silence stretched out between them. A cutting silence. Her future hung suspended in that silence.

Finally Abram sighed. "I will think about it."

His voice was still gentle. At least he had not rejected her request with finality.

But he had something more to say. He said it softly. "I'll pray about it."

That was what Hagar wanted to hear. "Thank you, Abram," she said. "Whatever God tells you to do, I will accept."

She rose to her feet, made a small bow, and left the tent.

In her tent she found herself gasping for breath. There was so much at stake here!

Her whole future! The predictions of Terah. The promises of Abram's God. Her own personal life! And she had done what she could. She had sown the seed in Abram's mind that this was God's will.

Now all she could do was wait. Wait for Abram to make his decision.

No. Wait for *God* to make his decision. Then tell Abram.

But in honesty, she didn't know whether she believed that or not.

19

The next day Abram offered a sacrifice. Following custom, he chose one of the best of his herd, a strong bullock which he offered to God. On a high place near the camp, he slit its throat, then burned it in the fire of the altar.

All day he stood there, watching the smoke rise in the clear sky. The men left him alone. Even Sarai, who had returned from visiting the king of Gerar, did not disturb him.

Hagar watched from a distance. She knew what was on his mind. A far-reaching decision. Her future. He was asking God to speak to him.

She snorted. More likely what was happening was that Abram was thinking it through. Debating in his mind the rightness and wrongness of the situation. Struggling with the facts and his common sense. When he reached his conclusion, he would announce God had spoken.

What would God say? That he had wronged his slave girl, and the baby would be hers? That she would be declared his *asha,* the mother of his descendants? Surely God would lead Abram — through his intelligence and sense of fairness — to the right conclusion.

From the doorway of her tent, she could see the scene in the distance — the lonely man, standing tall beside the burning altar, the smoke from the sacrifice rising. Toward God. This mysterious deity whom Abram insisted was real. A strange being who guided the ways of his people. Up there, out there — or in Abram's mind. Was he real? Or had Abram merely created a God for himself?

As evening shadows crept across the barren hills of the *negeb,* Abram returned to his tent. Had he made his decision? Had God spoken? Hagar considered going to Abram's tent to ask but discarded the idea. Sarai would be there. She would let Abram tell her when he was ready.

Hagar could not sleep that night. Shortly after she had gone to bed, she heard an argument in Abram's tent. Abram and Sarai must again be at odds. Abram, she hoped, was telling his wife of his decision to make Hagar his *asha;* Sarai was indignantly claiming her rights.

Hagar briefly considered barging into Abram's tent. But that would only add fuel to Sarai's wrath. Let Abram deal with Sarai. Eventually Sarai would accept his decision as God's will. And if the matter remained between her and Abram, she would be less likely to hold it against Hagar.

Hagar smiled as she settled into her bed. She was Abram's *asha.* His son would be *her* son, not Sarai's. The heir. Terah's deathbed prediction would be fulfilled.

Best of all, Abram would visit her tent. Not to sire a son, but because she was his *asha.* Everything good was happening to her. She could almost believe in Abram's God, who was treating her with justice and kindness. Now if only Abram's God would speak to her. . . .

The next morning when she awoke, she smiled and stretched lazily before rising. She was Abram's *asha.* Second only to Sarai in the household of Abram. And the child she was carrying inside her — yes, her son — was the heir to Abram and the promise he kept talking about.

Her son's future was bright. Many

descendants. Canaan for his homeland. Prosperity and wealth and luxury for all time to come. The day was sunny. Life was good.

"Hagar!"

Sarai was just outside her tent. The door flap lifted abruptly and Abram's first wife strode in. She did not remove her sandals. She strode across the carpet, leaving dusty footprints behind. She stood in front of Hagar, hands on hips, glaring at her.

"You pig!" Sarai's words barely concealed the hysteria behind her words. "You have poisoned my husband. After all I have done for you — "

"My lady," said Hagar. "Calm yourself. Please be seated. Let's talk — "

"I'll do the talking!" Sarai's fists clenched and unclenched. "I'll tell you what we decided. Last night. We talked about you and my son whom you're carrying in your belly. We decided that right after my son is born, you have to go. We keep the boy. You — *go!*"

"No, Sarai. We both stay. You are still the first wife, but I am the mother of Abram's heir. That is God's will. Didn't Abram tell you?"

"What?" Sarai's face at first registered surprise. Then she threw back her head and laughed. "I see now. You thought — " She sobered. "You have a lot to learn, slave."

"What do you mean?"

"I mean," said Sarai slowly, "that God spoke to Abram yesterday. And God told him that the child to be born to you is mine, as God promised. Did you think for a minute that God is so fickle he revokes his promises just because a slave girl asks it?"

"No!" Hagar could not accept what Sarai had just said. "You are wrong. God told Abram the child is mine! I am to be his *asha,* same as you — "

"No!" Sarai's face clouded. Then it softened. She gazed at Hagar, her lips pursed thoughtfully. "My dear, I understand now. You thought — Well, never mind. You were wrong. The child is mine. God has spoken."

It couldn't be. It just could not be. Sarai was wrong. Entirely wrong. Abram would tell her the truth.

Without bothering to finish dressing, Hagar pushed past Sarai and out of the tent. Barefoot and awkward in her swollen condition, she strode toward Abram's tent. He was not there. She looked for him. He was nowhere in sight. Breathlessly she ran up to the top of a nearby knoll and searched for him. At last! He was by a flock of sheep.

She seemed to carry a huge stone in her belly as she ran down the knoll in Abram's direction. Her running was more of a waddle. She held her belly with her hands to keep it from jiggling too much. After a few steps, she had to slow down to catch her breath. Stones on the ground cut her feet. By the time she reached Abram, she was walking — slowly lurching — toward him.

"Abram!" she gasped.

He turned, startled. Then he ran toward her, catching her as she was about to fall. She felt so weak, so dizzy. His arm went around her, supporting her.

"What is it, my child? What's wrong?"

"Is it true — " she gasped. "What Sarai said. . . ."

"Ah!" His arm tightened around her. "I told her not to talk to you. Not until I could tell you myself."

She wrenched away and stood swaying, glaring at him.

"Then it's true? What she said? The baby is hers?"

He nodded. "Please, child — "

"And after it is born, you'll take it away from me?"

He nodded. "Yes, but — "

"And then you'll send me away?"

"Hagar, listen! I didn't want it that way. But Sarai's right. You can't live here. It won't be as bad as you think — "

"No! No! You can't do this! Didn't God speak to you — "

"Yes, he spoke. Please understand. The child will belong to Sarai, as God promised. But as for you — "

But she turned and stumbled back toward the camp, her mind in a whirl. Abram had betrayed her. God had betrayed her. No, God had not spoken to him. Instead Sarai had twisted his thinking to have everything her way.

Her whole world, which had seemed so bright and happy just a few minutes ago, now was dark and stormy. Her life was destroyed. She was not Abram's *asha*. The child in her was not hers. There was no good God who ruled the lives of his people. He was no more than the moon goddess. No more than that donkey tethered there —

She stopped. She would take the donkey and flee.

She staggered to her tent, quickly packed bread and cheese into a blanket, put on her sandals, head covering and heavy cloak, grabbed a waterskin, and left. She placed her small bundle on the donkey's back and with great effort pushed herself up. It was a cruel load for the donkey, but she tapped it with her stick and the beast moved.

To the south. The road to Egypt.

She would go as far as the Well of the Antelope's Jawbone. There she would wait for a caravan. They passed through about every month, and there hadn't been one for a long time. It would come any day. She had enough food for several days, and there was water at the little oasis she was headed for.

She would go to Egypt. Directly to the royal palace at Zoan. There she would become the consort of the prince Senwosret. She would deliver her son, and he would be raised in the courts of the pharaoh. She would have other children, and the prince, the future pharaoh, would be their father. And she *would* be the mother of a great nation.

Furthermore, she would adopt the god of the pharaoh of Egypt. What was his name? Amun. Yes. She would pretend to believe in this god. He would direct her future. It didn't matter if he were real or not. No gods are real. None.

Especially that awful God Abram claimed to believe in.

20

The oasis at the Well of the Antelope's Jawbone was much farther than Hagar remembered it. Many years had passed since Abram led his family and flocks down the caravan road through the Wilderness of Shur toward Egypt. Hagar recalled the trip from Beersheba to Antelope's Jawbone as just a short easy stroll. But she was younger then, and not pregnant.

The back of the donkey had sharpened. Her weight bit into its ridge. Soon she was forced to slide off and walk. Walking was tiresome, even when she leaned on the donkey for support. She tried various positions on the beast's back, but nothing helped.

It was hot during this middle of the dry season. The sun beat mercilessly down upon her, and the dust swirled around her, clogging her nostrils. She felt gritty and damp. Her joints ached. Her mind went dull.

So did her backside. She forgot the pain caused by the donkey's spine. She closed her eyes, picturing the oasis at Antelope's Jawbone. A spring. Trees. Grass. Flowers. Sweet scents. Bird's songs. Cool breezes. An Eastern garden. Paradise. A place to sleep, to dream, to wait for a caravan to come to escort her to her future.

Would Abram follow her? He might. He wanted that child she carried inside her. He might come and capture her, drag her back bound hand and foot, take the baby from her womb, then send her out again by herself. She wouldn't let that happen. She'd hide at the oasis, and he would never find her.

She drifted off into dreams and fantasies during that interminable day. She was an Egyptian queen, and her son a prince. Sometimes she slept, although how she managed that on a donkey's back, she never knew. Sometimes she was half awake, half asleep. But she plodded on.

She wasn't even aware that they had reached the oasis until the donkey paused to drink. She sat slumped on the donkey's back and absently tapped it with her stick. The beast would not move. It continued drinking. Hagar opened her eyes and looked around. The oasis! The Well of the

Antelope's Jawbone! She had arrived.

The sun had gone down, and shadows wrapped the trees of the oasis. Instead of the green of her dreams, the color was gray. No flowers. No birds. No sweet scents. No lush garden. No sounds. Just the thirsty donkey drinking.

Slowly she slid down from the donkey's back. Her legs felt rubbery, but she managed to stagger to the edge of the pool. There she sank to her knees and plunged her face into the cool water. She drank. Then she removed her clothes and sponged off her hot sweaty body. She washed her clothes and put them back on damp, enjoying the coolness. She began to feel better.

She ate a few bites of bread, but a lassitude came over her. All she wanted to do now was sleep. She pulled the blanket around her and tried to settle herself.

Tomorrow she would find a hiding place. If Abram came, she would hide. No one was going to steal her baby from her. It was her baby. Hers alone. Terah had promised. The baby would be the father of a nation. And she would be the mother. In Egypt. Where there were many gods. Or no gods.

Sometime during the night, the first pain wakened her. A sharp stabbing pain. In her abdomen. She doubled up in the blanket, gritting her teeth. It soon passed.

What did it mean? Not labor pains. Impossible. The child wasn't due for another month. Muscle cramp possibly? That must be it. She tried to relax, to sink into the deep sleep and dreams of her future.

The second pain made her cry out. Another cramp. What caused it? Exhaustion? The water? The heat? Stiffness from her long trip?

When it passed, tears streamed down her cheeks. She could not face the possibility that her time had come. Not now! Not when she was alone! She could not deliver her own baby. No. It was muscle cramps. The heat. The cold. The sun. Or the moon. Anything. Not the baby!

When the third pain came, searing into her abdomen, she could no longer avoid reality. What should she do? She couldn't go back. She would have to stay here. The baby was coming. And she couldn't stop it.

Would the baby die? Would she die? Would —

Another pain. Intense, stabbing, piercing, lancing through her body like a hot knife. She tore at her clothes. Her scream startled the donkey.

"Help me! Somebody! Please help! *God!*"

But there was no God. Abram's God was

cruel, insensitive, unfeeling. And he certainly wasn't there. He was no more than Yarah the moon goddess, or the Egyptian Amun, or that awful Moloch who demanded that babies be burned. Moloch. Maybe he was the only god present, and he hungrily awaited her baby.

Ahhh-hhh-hhh!

The pain was more than she could bear. No one to help her. No human. No god. And the baby would not come.

She had watched births often enough to know that each was different. Some were easy, the baby sliding out gently after just a few short moments of little pain. Others were prolonged, lasting hours and even days, painful and torturous, accompanied by screams and moans and sometimes even death.

By the time the sun had reached the middle of the sky, she knew this birthing would be one of the difficult ones.

It went on and on. No relief. Her screams echoed around the little oasis. Getting weaker. She could feel her body weakening. She was dying. The baby was killing her. No. God was killing her. Abram's God. That horrid deity was killing her baby . . . killing her.

"God!" she screamed. "Ahhh-hhh-hhh!"

★★★

The place is no longer the *Well of the Antelope's Jawbone*. It is Beer-lahai-roi, *the Well of the Living One Who Sees. Birds sing. Bright flowers spangle the green grass, sweetening the light dry air. Breezes blow gently. The trees overhead give cooling shade.*

In this garden, Hagar feels no pain. She runs and dances and laughs. She sings songs of joy.

And God is there.

The name of the God is El-roi, *the God who sees. And he is speaking to her.*

"Hagar," says El-roi, *"what are you doing here?"*

She feels no fear, only a great peace. She turns to face him.

"Sir," she says, "I am running away from my mistress. She wants to steal my baby from me."

"Hagar," says the God, "return to your mistress and submit to her. Do all she tells you to do."

"Yes, El-Roi," *she replies.*

"Your son," the God continues, "will be like the wild ass. He will indeed be the ancestor of a great nation."

"Thank you."

El-roi *adds, "He shall be named* Ishmael, *for I have heard you."*

"Thank you, El-roi," *she repeats. "It shall be as you say. His name shall be* Ishmael."

And she says the name again. "Ishmael."

And again. "Ishmael." *And again.* "Ishmael . . . Ishmael . . . Ishmael. . . ."

Toward sunset, Abram and Mardi found her. They hurried into the clearing and knelt by the body of the *shifkhah*. She was unconscious then, her body dirty and drenched in sweat, her hair ragged and torn, her clothing in tatters.

The baby was half-born.

Abram and Mardi, although inexperienced in human births, knew what to do. They delivered the baby, cut the mother-cord, and washed baby and mother. Through it all, Hagar did not regain consciousness. She seemed to be in a delirium, muttering, stammering, murmuring.

Only one word came out of her which was audible and clearly discernible to Abram.

"Ishmael!" she cried. *God has heard!*

21

"Aunt Hagar! Look what I have!"

Hagar, who had just emerged from her tent, clapped her hands and shouted. "A *harye!* Good for you, Ishmael! Is that the one which has been killing the sheep?"

The young man nodded, his teeth flashing in a satisfied smile. "One arrow," he said proudly.

As usual, Hagar was more interested in the young man striding toward her than the lion he carried. She saw a boy — no, a young man, even though he was only fifteen. He was tall, muscular and handsome, his curly brown hair wreathing a sun-browned face. The stained leather tunic he wore was smeared with blood, some of it fresh.

"And where are Mardi and Eliazar?" she asked.

"Stalking a deer, somewhere in the Shur Valley. I thought I'd bring in the *harye* to show Father Abraham."

"And you killed the *harye* yourself?"

"Yes, Aunt Hagar."

She was not surprised. Although six years younger than Eliazar, and many years younger than Eliazar's father Mardi, Ishmael's skill as a huntsman was beginning to exceed theirs. He seemed instinctively to know the ways of forest creatures, and he could stalk a gazelle or wait patiently for an ibex. His powerful arms handled a bow easily. His arrows flew more accurately and farther than Eliazar's, and almost as powerfully as Mardi's. Yes, he would scorn the easy prey of the deer and go after the *harye* which had been harrying Abraham's flocks in the Shur Valley to the south.

"Father Abraham is in the near pasture to the north," said Hagar. "He'll be back at noon."

"Where's Mother?"

Hagar, with long practice, kept a smile. "She's in her tent." But despite her cheerful demeanor, the word "Mother" on the boy's tongue brought pain to her stomach.

She watched as the youth strode toward Sarah's tent, calling, "Mother! Come see what I've got!"

When Sarah emerged from the tent, she marveled at the fine kill her son had brought back from the wilderness. She also nagged him about his appearance, demanding he wash himself and put on a clean robe before his father returned at noon. Just like a mother.

Abraham and Sarah! For several years, she had found it difficult to call them by their new names. "Abraham," he had insisted, was the name God himself had given him. It was a much more appropriate name than Abram, which meant merely "Great Father." Abraham meant "Father of a nation." Now that he had a son and heir, he could claim that.

"Sarah," on the other hand, meant nothing new. "Sarai" meant "princess," and so did Sarah. But if Abraham had a new name, so must she.

And Hagar? Any name change there? Yes. She was now "Aunt Hagar," at least to Ishmael. Even so, their relationship was more like brother and sister.

From the time the boy was old enough to understand, he had been told that Hagar was his physical mother. He had accepted this as natural. She was the *shifkhah*. Her body had been used by Abraham and Sarah to produce a child. But that was all. Sarah was his real mother.

Hagar sighed as she went to the well to

draw water. It had been like this for fifteen years. Her breast milk had nourished the child until he was weaned, but that was as close as she was allowed to come to the baby. She recalled vividly the long nights as she lay sobbing alone in her tent, listening to the cries of the infant from Sarah's tent — wishing with all her heart she were the one who changed the swaddling cloths, treated his colic, and comforted the baby. *El-roi* had commanded her to "submit to her mistress." She had. But it wasn't easy.

Hagar could not convince herself that her vision at Beer-lehai-roi was real. It might have been just a product of her delirium. As time passed and El-roi did not again speak to her, she began to resume her skepticism about the reality of Abraham's God.

Never did she reveal her doubts to Abraham and Sarah. She spoke often and confidently of El-roi, "the God who sees her." She continued to call him that, although Abraham still called him *Elohim,* "the God of all Gods." Hagar had told them the full story of God's visit to her at the place she now called "The Well of the Living God Who Sees Me." Although Abraham was convinced that his God spoke to Hagar as much as to him, Sarah was doubtful.

"Are you *sure* God spoke to you?" she

often asked Hagar. It was as though she were saying, *You have schemed and connived and deceived Abraham in the past, but you never fooled me. I know you for what you really are.*

To Sarah, Hagar always displayed the utmost humility. El-roi's command to "submit to your mistress" made good sense. Otherwise, Sarah would have driven her out after baby Ishmael was weaned. Hagar submitted humbly, claiming it was El-roi's will. What she admitted to no one was that "God's will" meant the intelligent thing to do. She had learned that from Abraham.

Because of her submission, Sarah had reluctantly allowed her to stay. She no longer claimed her right to be Abraham's *ahsa*, and she acknowledged Ishmael as Sarah's child. To Sarah, she became the *shifkhah*, but Abraham accepted her once again as his daughter. Also, as Abraham said again and again, she was the one to whom God had appeared in a vision.

On her way back from the east well of Beersheba, the water jar she carried pressed down on her head. It seemed to get heavier every day. She knew why. She was thirty-four. Her body was not as strong as it was in those carefree days when she carried heavy loads on her head and back for long, long hours.

She would soon be past the time when she could bear children. Abraham and Sarah refused to consider a suitable marriage for her. They retained her as the *shifkhah*. If anything happened to Ishmael, their son and heir, she must be available for further childbearing. Again she felt like a ewe, an animal, whose body was used by her master and mistress for breeding purposes.

As she approached her tent, she saw Sarah still talking with her son. Still scolding. It had been like that for the past few years. Sarah, old and stooped and gray-haired, could not cope with a boisterous lad who always seemed to be doing something to displease her. No wonder he went hunting so often.

Sarah said something to Ishmael and pointed toward Hagar. The boy nodded, then turned and strode toward Hagar's tent, still carrying the harye on his shoulder.

"Aunt Hagar!" His voice held a petulant tone, perhaps from too much parental nagging. "Mother says I should skin this harye immediately, but I also have to clean up and change clothes immediately. Will you help me?"

Hagar knew how to turn the boy from a disagreeable mood to a pleasant one. She laughed. The brown face immediately brightened.

"Of course," she said cheerfully. "Over here, in the shade. You skin and I'll peel. And I want to hear all about your lion hunt!"

Under the welcome shade of the large oak tree, the two squatted on the ground and went to work.

"He's the same one, Aunt Hagar. Just last week he killed a sheep in the south pasture."

"Look how old he is, Ishmael. See his teeth? It must have been easy for you. The poor old dear." And she laughed again.

"Poor old dear nothing! This harye has been around long enough to learn a trick or two. I found his tracks near the Wadi Sheva four days ago, so we set up an ambush. But the smart old cat never came to drink while the three of us took turns. Finally Mardi and Eliazar went off looking for easier game, but I stayed. I got him early this morning."

"With one arrow?"

"Of course! Why would I need two?"

She laughed, trying to put a note of admiration into her laugh. He responded to her as always, with affection and companionship. She was neither his aunt nor his slave. She was his friend.

Ishmael slit through the remaining tendons as Hagar peeled the skin back. The boy looked up from his work, the brown face now suddenly serious.

"Aunt Hagar, why is Mother so mean all the time? I can't seem to do anything right any more."

"Be patient with her, Ishmael. She hasn't been feeling well lately."

The lad wiped off the bloody knife on his already stained leather tunic. "She's been that way ever since we moved down here from Hebron last month. Could it have anything to do with those three visitors we had?"

The three men who had enjoyed Abraham's hospitality in Hebron had told Abraham he could yet have another son, this time from Sarah's womb. Sarah had laughed, but Abraham took them seriously. Somehow he believed that God had spoken to him through the visitors.

"I don't know." Hagar began to scrape the bloody skin. "But one thing I do know. All that silly talk about your mother having a baby is nonsense."

"You're sure?"

"Yes, I'm sure. Sarah can't have babies any more. She's too old. You're their only baby, and she couldn't even have you!"

He smiled at this. "I guess I owe you something, Aunt Hagar. You gave me birth. You gave me your mother's milk. But — it's true, isn't it? I am Father Abraham's only heir?"

She nodded, ignoring the pain in her stomach. "Yes, Ishmael. You don't have to worry about that. You are Abraham and Sarah's only son. There will not be another."

Unless something happens to you. Then they'll have another. But not through Sarah. Through me.

She didn't say this aloud, but the thought must have been reflected in her face.

"Are you sure, Aunt Hagar? Somehow I get the feeling you don't entirely believe that."

Hagar took a deep breath, stifling the pain inside her. "It has to be, Ishmael. You are their heir. That's why your parents changed their names."

"Aw, I know about that. But how do you know those three men weren't really from God, like Father Abraham claims? Couldn't God make it possible for Mother Sarah to have a baby?"

"El-roi can do anything he wants. But why should he do that? It doesn't make sense. Abraham and Sarah already have an heir. And El-roi never does anything that doesn't make sense. You know that."

Ishmael nodded and rose to his feet in a lithe athletic motion. Hagar stood up more slowly.

"But Aunt Hagar. . . ." The boy's forehead

wrinkled in a puzzled frown. "What if it's true? What if Mother Sarah does have a baby? What would happen to me?"

Hagar laughed. "It can't happen. But if it did — " She sobered. Abraham's God, if real, could make it happen. But no. Never. El-roi was a figment of her delirium. Elohim was a product of Abraham's intelligence and observations. This God was a sane and reasonable creation of their minds. He would never do anything so — so *miraculous* as causing an old lady past her mother-time to have a baby!

If something like that happened, she might be tempted to believe that El-roi really existed. That he was truly the "God who sees her." That Abraham's "God of all Gods" was not just something he made up to explain everything. But no. That couldn't happen. Never.

She realized she was standing still, the skin of the harye still in her hands, staring blindly at a far mountain. And Ishmael stood before her, his face wrinkled with questions, waiting for her to finish what she had started to say. She had to say something. She spoke without thinking.

"If it did happen . . . then I guess you would be *my* son, instead of Sarah's!"

As soon as she said it, she bit her lip. She

wished she could take it back. Make it unsaid. But she couldn't.

The boy would be crushed by this answer. He was the son and heir of Abraham and Sarah. He would, like Abraham, be the "father of a nation." But as Hagar's son, he would be nothing.

To her amazement, the boy laughed. "Good!" he exclaimed. "That would be nice, to be able to call you 'Mother.' Now c'mon. Let's show that harye to Father Abraham."

"Not before you clean up, young man!"

"Aha!" Ishmael's laughter rang out. "You sound like a mother already!"

She joined his laughter, despite the pain in her stomach.

22

Sarah *was* pregnant!

It caught everyone by surprise — everyone except Abraham. He merely smiled and said, "Why not? Isn't that what those three visitors at Hebron promised?"

Sarah was fearful. "Having a baby at my age will kill me. Remember what happened to the Hurrian lady who gave birth after passing her drying-up time? She had a miserable experience and lived only four days afterwards."

Abraham only smiled. "The difference is that she was not under God's protection. You are."

Ishmael was devastated. "Father Abraham, if this is a boy, will he be the heir or will I? Am I your oldest son — or just the son of your *shifkhah?*"

Abraham's response was gentle. "Have no fear, my son. I will never disown you. You will receive half of my wealth when I die. You may dwell here forever with your brother. May there always be peace between you."

His answer was ambiguous. Half of Abraham's wealth would make Ishmael very wealthy. But Abraham's answer had avoided what he considered his son's main inheritance: the Promise. God had promised to make his descendants as the dust of the earth and the stars of the sky. Because of this nation, all people on earth would be blessed.

Hagar was confused. Terah had predicted — and El-roi confirmed — that Hagar's womb would be fruitful. Her son would be the father of a great nation. The three visitors at Hebron had promised that the boy from Sarah's womb would be the chosen one. Two contradictory predictions. Which was true?

Could a great nation descend from each of them? Then which would be the people of Abraham's God?

But Hagar had to confess to herself that what those three men told Abraham might have been a real word from Abraham's God. After all, the impossible had happened. Impossibly, Sarah had conceived in her old age. That was miraculous. And only God could make a miracle.

But wait. That wasn't entirely true either.

The Hurrian lady of whom Sarah had spoken had conceived in her old age. Perhaps others had done it also. Nothing miraculous about that. Unusual, perhaps. But a miracle?

She decided she would believe Terah's deathbed prediction, rather than that vague comment by the three strangers at Hebron. Everyone knew that the last words spoken by a dying man were prophetic. Yet she was honest enough to admit that she wanted to believe that Ishmael was the heir; maybe that was why she believed Terah's prediction.

Hagar felt uneasy about Sarah's pregnancy. Given the question about who was the true child of the Promise, she was in danger of being cast out, along with Ishmael. She would be nice to Sarah. She would not upset her, nor treat her as an equal. "Submit to your mistress," El-roi had said. Sound advice. The will of El-roi, her delirium-God.

"You must be gentle with your mother," she told Ishmael one day. "This isn't an easy time for her."

Ishmael frowned. "It's not an easy time for me, either. You know what happens to me if that baby is a boy."

"How do you know it will be a boy? What if it's a girl?"

Ishmael laughed, but without humor. "It's

a boy, alright. Mother wouldn't go to this much trouble to have a girl."

Hagar joined in his laughter, but she had noticed that everyone in the camp expected a boy. This was mostly because Abraham believed so strongly in the prediction of the three Hebron visitors.

"God keeps his promises," he said often, his voice firm.

Hagar privately wished the child would be a girl. Then Ishmael would continue to believe that Terah's prediction, not that of the three mysterious visitors, would be the true forecast of the future.

During the months of Sarah's pregnancy, Hagar made herself indispensable. She took over the major part of the work of the camp, freeing Sarah from large areas of responsibility. With Abraham's help, she arranged with the king of Gerar to have one of his midwives come to stay with them — the one known in the *negeb* for her experience and knowledge of medicine and herbs.

The midwife predicted that the delivery would be hard because of Sarah's age. She insisted Sarah be confined to her tent during the last month. She must lie down. No exertion. Nothing to do but sleep and eat. A light potion was prescribed. It seemed to relax the expectant mother.

When the time came for the baby's birth, only the midwife and Hagar were permitted in the tent. The delivery was much easier than expected, partly because of Sarah's relaxed condition and partly due to the midwife's skill. There was pain, of course. That was Mother Eve's curse, according to Abraham. But when it was over, Sarah was able to hold the baby in her arms.

"Father Abraham," called Hagar. "Come see your son."

Abraham stepped into the tent and automatically removed his sandals. He looked calm, as though the ordeal was no more than he expected.

"God be praised," he murmured as he knelt beside Sarah. "How are you feeling, my dear?"

Sarah smiled. "Tired but happy. We have a son!"

Abraham tenderly took the child in his arms. It was still wrinkled and slightly purple in color, but the boy seemed to move his hands and fingers with great energy. Abraham's face was glowing.

"This is the child of the Promise," he said.

Hagar, standing behind him, heard his words. The muscles in her jaw tightened. She clenched her fists. What did this portend for their future?

Sarah sat up in her bed, surrounded by cushions. She looked over at Abraham.

"Place the child on my knees," she said.

"Do you want to name him now?"

"Yes."

A naming ceremony usually took place a few days after the child was born. But there was no reason to put it off. Sarah seemed determined to do it immediately.

Gently Abraham placed the child on Sarah's knees and held it there. He looked at Sarah expectantly.

Hagar knew that in Abraham's family, the mother named the child. Sarah would probably select a name in keeping with the importance of her son. This was the heir of the Promise. His name should be meaningful.

"His name is Isaac," she said.

Hagar gasped. Isaac meant "laughter."

"Isaac?" Abraham's voice reflected surprise.

"Yes," Sarah smiled. She picked the child up and held it to her shoulder. "Once everyone laughed at me. Now I'm laughing. And everyone will laugh with me."

Abraham nodded. "Isaac it shall be." And suddenly he laughed. "Isaac. A good name. And may he grow into it!"

Hagar frowned. She could see nothing to laugh about.

Sarah's sagging breasts did not hold enough milk to sustain the new baby. Hagar arranged for a young mother with a two-month-old baby girl to come to Sarah's tent. Soon both babies were drawing milk together from the young mother's breasts.

Isaac appeared to be a healthy child. And he seemed to be growing into his name. The first indication of this came one day when Hagar placed the child in Sarah's lap.

Sarah smiled. "Hello, Little Laughter," she cooed.

The baby reached up and touched Sarah's face. Sarah kissed his hand and continued to talk softly. Then she laughed, coaxing a smile from the child. In a moment, the boy laughed. His first sound, other than crying.

"Little Laughter," said Sarah over and over again.

Hagar, watching, wondered if Isaac and Ishmael could grow up peacefully together. It was possible. If Isaac were indeed the good-natured youth his name augured, surely he would accept his older brother as equal.

But would Ishmael accept him?

In the few times she had talked to Ishmael, he had seemed insanely jealous of his new brother.

"He's taking my place, Aunt Hagar!" the youth protested. "What's to become of me?"

"Don't worry, Ishmael." Hagar placed her hand on his. "I've told you about Grandfather Terah's prediction. Nobody is going to take anything away from you."

"But which of us is Father Abraham's real heir?"

Hagar hadn't answered. The question hung in the air between them. They both knew Abraham had loudly proclaimed Isaac his heir.

Hagar watched the smiles exchanged by Sarah and Isaac, she remembered Ishmael's question: "What's to become of me?"

23

"Greetings, Mother. Have I missed the festival?"

Ishmael strode confidently into the clearing and marched — a little jauntily, Hagar thought — to where she knelt under the oak tree kneading bread. At seventeen, he was tall, broad-shouldered, and very — she searched for the right word — self-assured.

Without pausing in her work, Hagar smiled at him. "No, you haven't missed anything. It starts today. And don't call me mother. You know how Sarah feels about it."

Ishmael unshouldered the small deer and began to tie it to the rope dangling from a limb of the oak. He frowned.

"All right, Hagar, if that's what you want. But for the last two years I haven't felt like Sarah's son. Nor Abraham's, either."

Something of his bitterness was reflected in his words. It was there, Hagar knew. Since the birth of Isaac, he had increasingly turned away from his family, spending more and more time in the wilderness alone. Mardi and Eliazar no longer accompanied him on his hunting expeditions. Abraham's orders. It was as though Abraham were saying to his servants, *He's no longer my son and heir. Spend your time guarding and protecting my true son, Isaac.*

"Please, Ishmael, don't talk like that." Hagar glanced furtively around, but no one was near enough to hear. "You know your mother. If we aren't careful, she'll make us leave. She has already threatened that. We must be careful."

The youth snorted, tossing his head. The brown curls flopped over his forehead. "What difference would that make? I'm not living here any more anyway. I just drop in for the . . . *festivals!*"

His last word had a sharp sarcastic edge. The festival, which began today and would run for three days, celebrated the weaning of the baby Isaac. Several bulls had been slaughtered, and neighbors for many miles around Beersheba had been invited to come and celebrate. Even Abimelech, king of Gerar, had promised to attend.

Hagar had finished kneading the dough. Now she shaped it into a loaf for the oven.

As she wiped her hands on a towel, she looked up at the tall young man.

"Ishmael, just remember that if we are forced to leave, I will have no place to go. You do. But this is my home."

The boy grinned, his clean-shaven face bronze and shining. "Come live with me at the Wadi Sheva. I'll take good care of you. You can do all the cooking. And I'll even call you mother!"

Hagar laughed. "Cooking for you would be an endless job, with your appetite. But thanks for the invitation. It's nice to know I have somewhere to go when they turn us out."

Ishmael's handsome face suddenly grew serious. "Hagar, don't worry. I'll watch my tongue. I know how you feel about staying here. But I swear by my bow, I don't know why you want to stay. There's nothing for you here."

What Ishmael said was perfectly true. Hagar was thirty-seven now, and Abraham and Sarah had never made any move toward settling her in a suitable marriage. She would probably never have more children. Her work here in Abraham's tents consisted of managing the affairs of the household. She cooked, cared for children, kept the men suitably clothed, drew water and cut wood. Since Sarah had turned away from her, she had no close friends.

Yet the thoughts of leaving frightened her. She could go to live with Ishmael at his camp in the Wadi Sheva, but that would be a lonely existence. She could not go to Egypt. Senwosret — now pharaoh since the death of his father — would not remember her. And she was too old for his harem. There wasn't much else to do, other than stay here and work and live out her life in Abraham's tents.

At least Abraham was kind to her. He treated her as a daughter, indulging her, listening to her advice, often following it. He still clung to a remnant of his conviction that God spoke to him through her.

"Are you going to the festival?" she asked. She hoped he wouldn't. His bitterness might betray him, leading him to say something better left unsaid.

"I might." Ishmael grinned, flashing his even white teeth. "But only if you'll go with me."

"I have to stay here and smoke this deer which you just brought in — for which I thank you very much."

His grin turned into a frown. "That deer is for you, not the festival. I don't really care anything about those goings-on, and especially about the pretty smiles and cute sayings of the son and heir."

Hagar shook her head. "Either don't go to the festival, or wait for me. I'll go with you to make sure you behave."

"I think I'll wait for you. You're the only reason I came back here anyway. Besides, you need help with that deer." The edges of his mouth curled up, and his eyes twinkled. "Don't you, *Mother?*"

"Don't call me that, or I'll skin you along with the deer. Now sharpen that knife while I put this bread in the oven. I'll be right back."

She hurried toward the oven, where the fire had burned down to just the right temperature in the chamber above for baking. She must not forget about this loaf in the oven. Being with her son was so pleasant, she could easily forget to turn the bread. *Her son!* She must not call him that. She must not even think like that.

He was not her son. He was Sarah's.

Abraham had designated a broad oasis near the west well of Beersheba for the festival. He and Sarah dressed in their best linen robes as they entertained their guests. The three-day celebration would enable all his herdsmen and servants to come in at some time and partake of the feast.

Isaac was the center of attraction. The boy was dressed in a new robe Sarah had made herself. The expensive Egyptian linen had been dyed several colors, with red and blue dominating. Gold lace adorned the cuffs and hems. On his head he wore a blue and red headpiece with a gold band to hold it in place, although he obviously disliked it, constantly tearing it off and throwing it on the ground.

Isaac was not intimidated by the many guests who made him the center of attraction. He seemed to thrive on it. "Little Laughter" had grown into his name, and his cheerful disposition and bubbling laughter had endeared him to everyone he met.

As Hagar and Ishmael approached, Isaac was toddling around the crowd, saying "Mother" to all the women and "Father" to all the men. When the people laughed at him, he responded with giggles of his own. He also knew he would get a big laugh every time he tore off his headpiece and threw it down, as he was doing when Hagar and Ishmael approached.

"He's spoiled," muttered Ishmael into Hagar's ear.

"Hush." She went to the little boy, stooped down and spoke to him. "And how is the young man today?"

She picked up his headpiece and placed it on his head. The boy looked up at her, his eyes crinkled. Then with an exaggerated motion he swept it off and threw it to the ground. He giggled.

"No, Isaac. You mustn't do that. Now hold still!" Hagar struggled with the wriggling child as she tried to replace the headpiece. Meanwhile all around them the guests laughed at the boy's antics, which merely encouraged him.

"Here, let me do it." Ishmael squatted down beside the child.

"No, Ishmael — "

But Ishmael only smiled. "Hold still, little brother. Let me put this on you."

Gently he put the headpiece on, tightened the gold cord around it, and gave the boy a soft pat on his backside. "Now keep that on, young man." He laughed softly.

"Ish! Ish! Ish!" Other than "Father" and "Mother," this was the only name Isaac would say. It seemed so strange. He very seldom saw his older brother, yet he spoke his name and seemed to idolize him.

"Don't hurt him, Ishmael!"

These sharp words were spoken by Sarah, who had just come upon the scene. Hagar had not been aware of her presence. How long had she been there? If she had seen the whole byplay, she would know Ishmael had offered the child nothing but gentleness and affection. But perhaps Sarah had seen only that little slap on the boy's backside.

Ishmael stood and slowly turned toward Sarah. Hagar knew his hesitation was to control his emotions. By the time he faced his mother, his features were under control.

"I wouldn't hurt him, Mother. He's so cute! He reminds me of an otter."

It seemed natural that a man who lived in the wilderness would call a cheerful, playful boy an otter. Ishmael was obviously making every effort to be cordial to his mother.

But Sarah didn't take it that way. "Are you calling my son an animal?" she snapped.

"Why, no, Mother." Ishmael's eyes widened. "You see, an otter — "

"I think you'd better leave him alone," interrupted Sarah.

"All right, Mother." Ishmael paused only a minute, then turned and pushed his way through the crowd.

Hagar felt she should say something. "Please, Mother Sarah. Ishmael did not mean to — "

"I suppose you put him up to that!" Sarah's eyes flashed fire. Her lips were set in a firm line.

"Why, no. I — Oh, please — "

"Stop sniveling, *shifkhah*. And leave my son alone."

Hagar stared at her mistress, as the double insult began to make itself clear. This was the first time Sarah had called her *shifkhah* in many years. And the emphasis on *my son* was unmistakable.

"I'm sorry," Hagar muttered, and turned away.

She hurried through the suddenly sobered crowd of people to her tent. Where was Ishmael? She wanted to talk with him. He was nowhere around. Probably gone back to his tent — his home — at the Wadi Sheva.

She wondered what had sparked Sarah's anger. Was it the sight of Ishmael playfully slapping his little brother? Or had she heard the older boy's laugh and thought he was laughing *at* rather than *with* little Isaac?

Or was it the sight of Hagar and Ishmael together, standing tall and condescending over her little baby? Mother and son; Hagar and Ishmael. Mother and son; Sarah and Isaac. In Sarah's mind a wall had been built between the two pairs.

What would Sarah do about it? Hagar frowned. Were her days in Abraham's tents numbered?

She didn't have long to find out. That

night Abraham came to her tent.

"Hagar, my daughter."

Abraham stood just inside the tent flap, removing his sandals. His hair and beard were neatly combed and oiled. Except for the use of the term "my daughter," Abraham reminded her of those two blissful months almost eighteen years ago when he had come to her tent. But she knew the purpose of this visit was not going to be as pleasant.

"Please be seated, Father Abraham. May I pour you some wine?"

"Thank you, my child."

There was silence between them for the moment it took to pour the wine into a cup and hand it to him. She sank to a cushion and looked at him anxiously.

Finally Abraham sighed. "I'm sorry, my dear. But you will have to go."

She nodded. There was no surprise in this. She had half expected it all day. She was determined not to show her anger and disappointment to Abraham.

"I meant no harm today, Father. Neither did Ishmael. We were gentle with the child, and we only played with him."

"I know, Hagar. But Sarah. . . ."

He stroked his beard, his fingers uncharacteristically nervous. He seemed to be struggling for the right words.

"It wasn't only what happened today. Sarah feels so insecure when Ishmael comes around. And as for you — "

"Yes, I know. I have sensed her dislike of me for several years. She — she thinks I'm a threat to her position as your wife."

Abraham nodded. "I'm glad you understand. You must know how I feel about you."

"I do."

"And you must know that you and Sarah cannot continue to live together in my tents."

"I know."

"And so I'll have to send you away."

"I understand."

Abraham breathed a sigh of relief. "Thank you for that. This is very difficult for me, to have to tell you this."

"I know."

"And I shall always love you, my daughter."

"Your love will always be returned, my father."

The deliberate use of "my daughter" and "my father" left much unsaid. Their eyes met. No further words were necessary.

Abraham rose to his feet and reached for his sandals. "If you like, I'll send you to Egypt with that caravan encamped at the south oasis. I'll give you a large dowry and arrange — "

"No, Father Abraham. That won't be necessary. I'll go to live with Ishmael."

"Ishmael?"

She smiled. "He is my son, you know."

"Will he have you?"

"Just this morning he invited me."

"And what can I give you? Servants? Goats? Cattle? Sheep? Gold?"

"Nothing, Father. Just a donkey and enough food and water to get me to the Wadi Sheva."

"Do you know how to get there? Suppose I send Mardi — "

"No, Father Abraham. I'll go alone. And I'll leave early tomorrow morning."

"So soon?"

"It's better that way."

"Yes." He stood there at the flap of the tent, staring at her. His eyes were tender and sad.

"I'm sorry, daughter."

"I know, Father. It's all right."

"Yes. It is. Because it's God's will."

With these words it seemed the love and affection binding them together disintegrated. God's will! Always that God of his!

She struggled to keep her feelings from being reflected in her facial expression. Abraham seemed not to notice the change in her.

"I'll see you tomorrow then. At dawn."

As the tent flap closed behind him, she stood there, a coldness seeping through her body. In spite of the love she felt for Abraham, she would be glad to go. There was nothing left for her here. There was only Isaac, the true son and heir of Abraham, who all his life would be laughing at her. There was Sarah, who would give her nothing but anguish and misery. And there was Abraham, the only one who cared for her, but who would give her nothing but a constant diet of "God's will."

She would go, she thought angrily. She would leave Abraham to his God. Then Abraham's Elohim could work his will with Abraham all he wanted.

Stay here in Beersheba, Elohim. Or El-roi or whatever you choose to call yourself! Don't follow me to the Wadi Sheva. I want nothing more to do with you!

24

The caravan route Hagar followed toward the southeast offered easy traveling, in spite of the heat of the day. She alternated between riding and walking, recalling another trip almost eighteen years ago when she had fled from Sarah in another direction to Beer-lehai-roi. Only then she had been pregnant.

When should she turn south to find the Wadi Sheva where Ishmael had pitched his tent? She had never been this way before. It would be easy to get lost. And this wilderness was not a good place to get lost. The landscape was barren, filled with rocks, sand, sharp crags, and no water. She was grateful for the large skin of water Abraham had thoughtfully given her this morning when she started out.

Abraham had kissed her lovingly this morning, although it was a father-daughter kiss, unlike the ones she so vividly remembered eighteen years ago. He had renewed his offer of a dowry. Again she refused. He had asked her to return to visit, but she had obstinately declared she would never come to his tents again as long as Sarah was alive. They had parted with tears and assurances of love.

Abraham had worried about the pillar of smoke they could see on the horizon to the southeast. She wondered if there was a forest fire, but Abraham said there were no forests in that direction. It seemed to be coming from the Siddim Valley, and Abraham warned her not to go near there. Perhaps King Chedorlaomer had gone to war again.

That pillar of smoke was still there. As she plodded on, hour after hour, the smoke grew thicker and wider on the horizon. What was happening in the towns of Gomorrah and Sodom? Would Abraham have to go rescue Lot again?

As evening approached, she became concerned about where to turn south to find the Wadi Sheva. She could not find the landmarks Abraham had told her about — the pointed mountain to the south and the ancient terebinth tree at a bend of the road. She had hoped to meet a traveler to ask but had seen no one.

Now there was someone. A woman. There, under the escarpment to the north. She was gathering wood.

Taking a firm grasp on the donkey's rope, Hagar turned toward the woman. She could get directions to the Wadi Sheva, and perhaps even spend the night in the tent of this woman's family. Desert hospitality would never be denied a traveler.

The woman paused in her work to watch Hagar approach. She was young. Very young. Hardly more than a girl. Maybe the daughter of a lone shepherd here in the wilderness. Or someone's servant.

"Who are you, and what do you want?" the girl demanded in a sharp voice. Desert hospitality?

Hagar stopped twenty steps away, uncertain. "I . . . I'm a lone traveler, trying to find the Wadi Sheva. Can you direct me?"

The girl shook her head, saying nothing.

"Please." Hagar tried not to sound like she was begging. "Will you offer me the hospitality of your tent for the night? I promise I'll be on my way tomorrow morning."

The girl stared at Hagar for a moment, her eyes cold. Finally she sighed. "I suppose I'll have to. Follow me."

She shouldered her pile of wood and turned to follow a small trail up the hillside.

Hagar followed. The donkey had some trouble on the steep path, but finally they emerged on a level area just below the escarpment. Hagar could see a small cave in the wall of the cliff.

"My father is sick," the girl said. "My sister and I have to take care of him."

"May I help? I know a little bit about illnesses — "

She stopped as another girl came out of the cave. An older girl. She looked vaguely familiar. The way her hair fell over her prominent forehead —

Lot's daughter!

Several years had passed since Lot's last visit, and the girl then was only a few years old. But that forehead was unmistakable. She was now in her teens, possibly early twenties, but it was the same girl.

Then the man in the cave —

Hagar stood tall and calm before this frowning lady.

"May I see your father? I know him. He is Lot ben Haran, nephew of Abraham. And he knows me."

Behind her, the younger girl gasped, and the older girl frowned. "How did you know — "

But Hagar took advantage of their astonishment and pushed past her into the cave.

It took her a moment to adjust her eyes to the darkness of the cavern. Before she did, she identified a smell. The sweet, sick smell of wine. She had smelled it before. One of Abraham's servants occasionally got drunk, and he often smelled like this. Abraham did not allow his servants to drink too much beer or wine, because it usually made them sick and irresponsible. Soon this cave would have another smell — the nauseating stink of vomit.

As her eyes adjusted to the gloom, she saw him. He lay propped against a stone. The wineskin lay in reach. He was staring at her.

"Hagar!" he muttered.

Lot had aged. He was not much older than she, but he looked like an old man. She couldn't see clearly, but she thought his hair and beard were streaked with gray. And she did identify age lines on his face.

He was disheveled. His beard and hair were not combed and oiled. His clothes were soiled. He was drunk.

She knelt beside him. "How are you, Lot?"

He grinned. "Did you come to lie with me, *shifkhah?* You're just in time. My wife is dead."

Baara! Hagar recalled the pretty young wife who had seemed so vivacious. Dead. Perhaps that explained his drunken behavior.

"No, Lot. I won't lie with you." She tried to keep the disgust out of her voice. "I merely want directions to Wadi Sheva. I'm going to live with Ishmael now."

"Ishmael!" He said it with a sneer. "The disinherited son of Abraham. A wild ass of a man. Hah! You'd be better off with me. Yes. I'll even marry you, *shifkhah*."

Questions flashed into her head, but she shoved them aside. All she wanted to do now was get out and be on her way, even if it was growing dark.

"Just tell me where to find the Wadi Sheva, Lot."

He hiccupped. "Don't know. Never heard of it. Ask Ishmael. The wild ass!"

That was the second time he had called Ishmael a "wild ass." The *aram* was often used symbolically to describe somebody who lived alone in the wilderness. She vaguely remembered that someone else had called him that, but she could not recall who.

Lot continued to stare at her. "Or ask those two men. They'll tell you. Yes. They'll tell you everything!"

Hagar frowned. What was he talking about?

"What two men?" she asked.

"*Those* two men. They came to me in Sodom. Then they told me to go. 'Go fast,' they said. Sodom was going to be destroyed."

"Who were they, Lot?"

"I don't know. Just two men. Maybe God sent them. They sure knew what they were talking about! Sodom — everything burned. . . ."

Hagar felt a chill in her spine. That pillar of smoke she had watched all day! Sodom burning? What horrible things must be happening over there!

"Did you say two men? Where are they now?"

"Don't know. Gone. Said they wouldn't destroy Zoar. Smoke. Lots of smoke."

Two men. She remembered the three men who had visited Abraham at Hebron. Could it be. . . ?

Lot seemed to be drifting off in an alcoholic stupor. She couldn't stay here. For what little daylight remained, she would have to move on. Find a place to stay overnight. Then go on in the morning. Maybe she could find someone who would direct her to the Wadi Sheva.

Lot roused himself and reached for the wineskin. "Stay with me, Hagar. Need a wife. Got no sons. Only daughters. Stay."

The wine spilled on his robe.

Hagar hurriedly left, pushing past the two girls who merely stared at her. Hagar saw fear in their eyes. Did they think she was a witch? Just because she knew who Lot was?

Carefully she led the donkey down the steep path and came to the road again. Her water was almost gone. The night would be cold, but she had a good blanket. And food. But she would have to find the Wadi Sheva soon.

She found a place to stay that night. A rock overhang. Not exactly a palace, she thought grimly, but shelter. She ate some bread and cheese and shared her remaining water with the donkey. Then she curled up in her blanket and tried to sleep.

Two men.

Had Abraham's God gone to the Valley of Siddim? Why? Was it he who had caused destruction? She shuddered. If so, then somehow he had saved Lot. And his two daughters. But not Baara. Lot's wife had evidently been destroyed in the . . . whatever was happening to Sodom.

Two men. . . .

In the morning she resumed her journey.

The sun seemed to Hagar to intensify as the day progressed. She and her donkey had

had no water since the night before. They had to find the Wadi Sheva — soon.

Toward the east dust and haze and smoke obscured the horizon. She could see the air in the distance shimmering, blurring the landscape. No trees. No green vegetation. Nothing but rocks and sand and hills, and the endless caravan trail leading toward that smoke smudge still visible in the southeast.

She now walked beside the donkey, holding its neck for support. Their pace grew slower and slower, and it seemed as though they were both staggering. Plodding on. Step after step. Her tongue began to swell in her mouth.

Something moved on the road ahead. She shaded her eyes and stared, but all she saw was a shimmering blur. The blur gradually took shape. A man. A lone man. Walking toward her.

Would he have water? Would he share it with her?

The man approached, striding vigorously. He was dressed in the long woolen robe and headpiece worn by most people in the land of Canaan. His heavy brown beard showed streaks of dust and sweat, but his face, though dusty and wet with sweat, was strong and young-looking.

Hagar and the donkey stood still, but the

man came forward and stopped before them.

"Greetings, mother." His voice was courteous.

He showed respect by calling her mother. The more common title would be woman, daughter, or grandmother — depending on the age of the person addressed. That he had chosen "mother" showed courtesy. Still Hagar wondered why that particular term.

She bowed her head before him. "Please, sir. . . ." But her word came out as a croak, hurting her dry throat.

Without a word the man unslung the waterskin from his shoulder and handed it to her. No water ever tasted sweeter. She paused for breath and was about to drink again when his hand on her arm restrained her.

"Not too much," he said softly. "You'll have a stomach ache. Besides, it's your donkey's turn."

He led her to the patient donkey's head and cupped his hands. She poured water into them, and the donkey lapped it eagerly. She began to feel better as her body responded to the moisture it had been lacking.

"Thank you very much, sir," she murmured.

"Are you going far?" His voice showed concern.

"The Wadi Sheva. Can you direct me?"

The man stared at her for a moment, his dark eyes kind. He spoke softly. "You must be Hagar the Egyptian."

She gasped. "How did you know?"

She never called herself "the Egyptian" any more. She was "Hagar, *bas bayit* of Abraham." But with a start she realized she could not call herself that now. She might as well be "Hagar the Egyptian."

The man smiled. "I have just come from the Wadi Sheva, where I talked with your son Ishmael." He grinned. "He's living there like a wild ass."

The phrase as he used it was not un-complimentary. It was merely a commentary on how well Ishmael had adapted to a solitary wilderness life, like the *aram*. The name had a familiar ring to it. Oh yes — Lot had called him that. Lot used the term jealously. This stranger used it respectfully. But somewhere, sometime ago, she had heard the term before.

The stranger continued. "He is expecting you."

"But how would he know — ?"

"He didn't, really. But he told me your story. He guessed that Sarah would insist that you leave. If that happened, he knew you would come here." The man grinned.

"You know, I've seen you before."

"Where have we met, sir?"

"At Hebron. I visited Abraham's tents a few years ago, and saw you there. You served me wine."

The man must have a good memory. Certainly better than hers. She could not remember him.

"Is my son well?"

"He is well, mother. He told me of Terah's prediction. I'm sure it will be fulfilled in Ishmael. But he will need a wife. I suggest you find him one, possibly from Egypt."

"Thank you sir. I must go to him now. Is it far?"

"Not far at all. Just walk down the road half a mile, and you will come to a terebinth tree. Turn south, and walk toward the mountain which has a sharp peak. Soon you will come to the Wadi Sheva. Follow it eastward until you come to Ishmael's tent."

"I am eager to see him again. And I'm grateful to you for your kindness."

The man shouldered his waterskin. "Good-bye, Hagar the Egyptian. El-roi go with you." He strode toward the northwest.

Hagar touched the donkey. Together they began the slow trek over the last few miles to the Wadi Sheva. It wasn't until they had reached the terebinth tree, gnarled and weatherbeaten, that what the stranger had said last penetrated her numbed mind.

El-roi!

No one ever called God that. No one but she. A few times she had talked about God's name to Abraham. Maybe Abraham had told this man several years ago when he visited the patriarch's tents. If so, he must have a remarkable memory.

She turned and searched for him in the shimmering distance. Yes, there he was, striding along purposefully. As though sensing her eyes on him, he turned and waved. Then he continued his journey, until his image was lost in the dust and haze of the barren landscape.

One man.

She shook her head, bewildered. He had given her the blessing of *El-roi,* the God of her delirium at Beer-lehai-roi. *El-roi.* "The God Who Sees Me."

One man.

Had she at last met Abraham's God face to face?

25

"Greetings, Hagar, my daughter."

"Father Abraham, it's good to see you again."

Abraham and Hagar embraced. He placed a tender kiss on her cheek. More than thirty years had passed since Hagar had left Abraham's tents. She had fulfilled her vow not to return again as long as Sarah lived.

The thirty days of mourning were over. Sarah's body lay in the new tomb of Macpelah, recently purchased from the local inhabitants for the family burial lot.

Hagar stepped back and looked at Abraham. "You're looking well, Father."

The aging patriarch stood erect and strong, his white hair and beard oiled and combed now that the mourning period had passed. His skin was smooth, and his eyes under heavy white brows keen and piercing.

"Thank you. And have you been well, my dear?"

"Yes, Father. Quite well. And happy. I am the grandmother of a new nation."

"So I have heard. Ishmael, the mighty hunter of Paran. He has quite a reputation, not only for the quiver full of arrows he shoots at wild game, but also those he shoots from his marital quiver!"

Hagar laughed. It was good to exchange witticisms with Abraham again.

"And you, Father? It seems your quiver is not empty."

She glanced at the women who had gathered outside Abraham's tents at Hebron to see the fabled visitor from the Wilderness of Paran. They were all strangers to Hagar. But she knew one was Abraham's young wife Keturah, mother of six sons born to the patriarch in old age.

Abraham followed her glance and smiled. "You'll meet them later. Right now I want to talk with you."

He placed his arm around her shoulders and led her away, turning his back on his family. This, Hagar interpreted, was a distinct honor. It was a sign of his love for her that he would want a few moments alone with his adopted daughter whom he had not seen for over thirty years.

He led her up a familiar path toward a hilltop which brought back many memories for Hagar. A moment later, they crested a hill overlooking the camp. Below they could see the cluster of tents and the group of women in the clearing, now chatting among themselves. Waiting for Abraham to come down.

Always waiting for Abraham.

How many times had they done that? He had often gone into the mountains alone, to talk to his God. And they had waited. Waited for God to speak to him. And he had always come back, and told them what was God's will.

"And how is your son, Father Abraham?"

The old man's alert eyes bored into hers. The question was subtly phrased. She knew he had two sons. But only one was the child of the Promise. Abraham's pause before answering indicated that he understood her subtlety.

His answer was also careful. "Of the fortunes of one son, you know better than I. Of the other . . . Isaac is doing well. Soon I will send to Haran for a wife for him. Some day both my sons will fill the earth with the descendants of Abraham."

Hagar nodded. "And the sons of Isaac will fulfill the Promise of Elohim."

Abraham grinned. "As the sons of Ishmael will fulfill the promise of El-roi."

They laughed as understanding flowed between them. The same God, known to them by different names. The same promise, although the one made to Abraham was slightly different. Each would be ancestor of a great nation. But only one had been told, ". . . and through this nation, all people on earth will be blessed."

"God be praised!" murmured Hagar.

Abraham instantly sobered. "And now, my daughter, do you believe in this God?"

She looked up into his eyes. Those honest, sincere eyes, so filled with integrity and faith. How much should she tell him? The truth, of course. The whole truth. She had never told anybody before — not even Ishmael — because of the doubts which had swirled in her mind through the years.

"I met him, Father. The day after I left your tents thirty years ago. I met El-roi on the way to the Wadi Sheva."

"Aha!" Abraham shouted. He smashed his fist into his open palm. "Tell me about it, my dear!"

"He was only a man, Father. A plain, ordinary-looking traveler whom I met on the road."

"And yet you knew who he really was?"

"No. Not at first. I thought he was just another Canaanite, probably a shepherd."

Abraham nodded. "I believe you. God usually doesn't reveal himself in spectacular ways. What did he say? Did he tell you who he was, or say anything unusual?"

"No. That's what caused my doubt at first. He only said he believed Terah's prediction would be fulfilled. But he didn't say he would *make* it happen."

"Yes." Abraham nodded slowly. "He left you room to doubt — so you could never be sure. Is that right?"

"Yes. For many years I was unsure it was truly El-roi."

"But now?"

She smiled. "How can I believe otherwise? I see Ishmael and his sons. I see Isaac, who will soon have sons of his own. And most of all, I see you, and your great faith. How can I not believe?"

Abraham stroked his smooth white beard. "Ah, the wisdom of age. You are not the skeptical little girl I knew."

They were silent for a moment, gazing out into the valley and the distant wooded hillsides. With the passing of the *malkosh*, the sun beamed down upon them. The air was sweet and clean now that the rainy season was over.

Hagar sighed. "Father Abraham," she said slowly. "When I was young, I used to ridicule your faith. I thought it was silly."

"I know, my child. I was well aware of that."

"You were?"

"Of course. But no matter. It's not the opinions of others that determine the depth of my faith."

"I know, Father."

Abraham reached out his hand for hers. "Come live with me, my daughter. You are welcome in my tents now."

She smiled up at him. "No, Father Abraham. I cannot. My home is with my son. And his family. We will move to Punon soon, and there we will settle. My destiny is with him, not with you."

He gazed at her steadily for a moment. Finally he spoke, his voice low.

"Yes. You are right. That is God's will."

God's will! At one time she would have scoffed at this, but not now. She sighed. Somewhere behind her, a bird sang in a tamarisk tree. Singing about life.

"El-roi bless you, my father."

"Elohim bless you, my daughter."

Together they walked down the hill toward the waiting people below.

The employees of Thorndike Press hope you have enjoyed this Large Print book. All our Large Print titles are designed for easy reading, and all our books are made to last. Other Thorndike Press Large Print books are available at your library, through selected bookstores, or directly from us.

For information about titles, please call:

(800) 223-1244

To share your comments, please write:

Publisher
Thorndike Press
P.O. Box 159
Thorndike, Maine 04986